Open
Secrets

Open Secrets

Jennifer Manuel

James Lorimer & Company Ltd., Publishers
Toronto

James Lorimer & Company Ltd., Publishers acknowledges funding support from the Ontario Arts Council (OAC), an agency of the Government of Ontario. We acknowledge the support of the Canada Council for the Arts, which last year invested $153 million to bring the arts to Canadians throughout the country. This project has been made possible in part by the Government of Canada and with the support of Ontario Creates.

Cover design: Tyler Cleroux
Cover image: Shutterstock

Library and Archives Canada Cataloguing in Publication (Paperback)

Title: Open secrets / Jennifer Manuel.
Names: Manuel, Jennifer, author.
Series: SideStreets.
Description: Series statement: SideStreets
Identifiers: Canadiana (print) 20200356607 | Canadiana (ebook) 20200356674 | ISBN 9781459415881 (softcover) | ISBN 9781459415898 (EPUB)
Classification: LCC PS8625.A69 O64 2021 | DDC jC813/.6—dc23

Published by:
James Lorimer &
Company Ltd., Publishers
117 Peter Street, Suite 304
Toronto, ON, Canada
M5V 0M3
www.lorimer.ca

Distributed in Canada by:
Formac Lorimer Books
5502 Atlantic Street
Halifax, NS, Canada
B3H 1G4

Distributed in the US by:
Lerner Publisher Services
241 1st Ave. N.
Minneapolis, MN, USA
55401
www.lernerbooks.com

Printed and bound in Canada.
Manufactured by Friesens in Altona, MB in December 2021.
Job #284806

For my dear friend, Helen Jones, whose unflinching commitment to sexual education promises a safer future for children.

Chapter 1

Open Mic Night

The second the doors of the Showcase opened, I hurried into the music café. Other musicians bumped into my guitar case as we crowded in. We all put our gear in the designated area. I grabbed a slip of paper from the front counter. On it I scribbled down the name of our band: *Shadow Beat*. Then I dropped the paper into the white bucket hanging on the wall. It was surrounded by framed photographs of famous musicians.

One day my picture would be up there. Signed, *Ana "Shadow" Santos*.

Right now there were only musicians and the baristas behind the counter. But in half an hour the place would be packed. My heart was already racing with the hope of getting picked tonight. Finally our chance.

I sat at a table and waited for my band to arrive. At the other end of the café, the stage was set up with mic stands and drums. Plus a keyboard and two giant amps. Nothing excited me more than the sight of music gear.

"Great outfit!"

I looked down at my outfit. Everything black. Like a shadow. A black shiny shirt that fit tight. Fake leather pants with knee-high boots over top. Then I twisted around to see who had spoken.

The man introduced himself. "Gill Daring."

My stomach fluttered. *Of course you're Gill Daring*, I thought. *Who doesn't know that?*

Gill Daring was the owner and manager

of the Showcase. Gill Daring had the power to make or break new bands. Gill Daring had his arm wrapped around every musician in the photographs on the wall.

He walked around to the other side of my table. "And you are?"

Blown away that you're talking to me, I thought. I almost forgot my own name for a second. Then I said, "Ana Santos. But I go by Shadow on stage."

I could see other musicians staring at Gill. I smiled to myself. Every one of them would kill to be me right now.

Gill sat across from me. "You must be new to Open Mic Night."

Play it cool, I told myself. I tried not to stammer. "My band has come to every Open Mic Night for the last seven months. But we've never been picked."

Gill flashed a big smile. His perfect white teeth could blind a person. "What do you play, Ana?"

"Guitar. And I'm an electronic music producer. I create my own sounds that I add to our live stuff." Talking about my music calmed me down a little.

Gill squinted one eye. "How old are you?"

I flinched. Was there an age limit I never knew about? The Showcase wasn't a club. It was a coffee shop that put a spotlight on local bands.

"Seventeen," I said.

"So you're — what? In grade eleven?"

"Twelve."

"Ah, graduation year." He chuckled, then crossed his arms casually. "I bet your parents want you home studying. Instead of here playing music."

"My parents don't have much to say about anything," I said. It wasn't fair of me. It made them sound like they didn't care. "They're in Mexico. They have a new business down there."

"Guess they're away a lot, then?" he asked. "Must be hard on you."

I lived with my older brother, Jose. But I decided to leave that part out.

"My best song is called 'Fiercely Independent.' It's my personal anthem," I said. "I'm used to taking care of myself."

"I can tell." He leaned back and ran his fingers through his thick black curls. "So, you got big plans for yourself, Ana Santos? In music, I mean."

Now was not the time to be shy. "Big plans," I said confidently.

He motioned at the stage behind him. "So this is your dream?"

"Definitely," I said.

"Your biggest dream? A dream you'd do anything for?"

"Going to give it everything I've got," I said.

Gill rose from his seat. "I can't wait to hear your band tonight."

I crossed my fingers. "If we get picked."

Open Mic Night was a lottery. Luck of the

draw. With so many bands hoping for a spot, the odds weren't high.

Gill started to walk away. Then he turned and winked at me. "I have a good feeling."

My heart pulsed faster. What did he mean by that? Every band was supposed to have an equal chance of being picked. But I was no fool. I knew that a guy like Gill Daring could probably do whatever he wanted.

Before I had a chance to think about it, the rest of Shadow Beat arrived. Harold Fox, my best friend since fifth grade, spun his drumsticks around his fingers. Our keyboardist, Yannick Ferreira, bobbed his head in his gold-coloured headphones. Isaac Johnny walked his bass guitar through the crowd to set it in the corner next to my guitar. Trey Habermas, our lead singer and rapper, wore his lucky ball cap — the black one with a peace sign stitched in bright green.

"Can't wait to sit here drinking coffee for five hours again. Watching crappy bands," Isaac said when he returned. "Waste of time. We never get picked to play on Open Mic Night."

Isaac was a grouchy old man inside a teen's body. "It'll be worth the wait," I promised. "We're really good. You know we are. Just wait until people get the chance to hear us. Big things will happen."

"That's right," Trey said. "I've been working on some new lyrics. Best bars I've ever written. Like, next level stuff. Once Ana puts down the riffs and chords for it, plus beats from Harold, we're looking at instant hits."

Just then, the café dimmed. The stage filled with coloured lights. The loud talk at the tables hushed. Gill Daring strolled onto the stage with the white bucket in his hand. Seeing him from a bit of a distance, I guessed he was in his late twenties. I looked around the place and noticed quite a few women in the crowd checking him out. He *was* pretty good-looking.

"You know what's in here?" he asked the crowd. "Your shot at being discovered. Once

I call the name of the first band, they've got eight minutes to set up their gear. No more than three songs." He reached into the bucket and pulled out a slip of paper. "Our first lucky band to perform tonight . . ."

The whole café fell silent.

"Shadow Beat!"

Chapter 2

The Next Big Sound

Eight minutes. That's how long we had to set up our gear. Hundreds of times I'd plugged the cables into my gear. I knew it like the back of my hand. Of course, when it mattered most, I fumbled to get the inputs and outputs set up. I tried to steady my hands. *Don't mess it up*, I thought.

I plugged my Fender guitar into the giant amp and turned it on. A loud hum droned from the speaker. Normally that sound made my skin prickle with excitement. But this time, I couldn't stop thinking about all the eyes on the stage.

On me.

My stomach turned queasy. Stage jitters.

I told myself to shake it off. Then I remembered. I was not Ana on stage. I was Shadow. And Shadow wasn't scared of anything.

In the middle of the stage, Trey adjusted the height of his mic stand. His hands were trembling. That made me even more anxious. If our lead singer couldn't command the stage, we would lose the audience by the first chorus.

I set down my electronic groove pad on the tall speaker next to me. With the touch of its buttons, my groove pad played the extra beats and special effects in our songs. I created them all myself. It was what made our sound special.

I took a deep breath and shook out my hands to keep them loose. No way could I shred the fretboard if my muscles were tense.

Two minutes left. Plenty of bands had been kicked off the stage for not being ready to play on time. Turning my back to the audience, I gave a quick nod to the others. Isaac already had his fingers dangling over the bass strings. He nodded to me that he was good to go, but I could see worry in his eyes. Harold also returned my nod as he wiped sweat from his forehead. Even Yannick, who was the calmest person I had ever met, looked uncertain.

Guess it's up to me to give this band some confidence, I thought. *We've been practising every night for this moment. We can't blow our big chance.*

I stepped up to my mic. "Thank you, Showcase! My name is Shadow. This is Shadow Beat, and our first song is called 'Contagious'!"

I pressed a button on my groove pad. A crunchy growl rumbled out of the speakers. It grew louder and louder, then broke down into a glitchy stutter. As the sound faded away, I strummed power chords on my guitar. The rhythm was fast and punchy. Several people in the crowd started to move their heads to the music.

Harold added a kick drum beat. That was Trey's cue to grab the mic.

"Baby you so contagious," Trey rapped, but his first line came out weak.

My stomach tightened. *Come on, Trey, you can do this.* Smiling, I tried to flash him a look of encouragement.

Trey delivered the next line perfectly. "Even doctors say you is outrageous."

From that point on, Trey was unstoppable. All eyes were on him as he twisted his cap sideways and pointed his hand up and down in time with his rhymes. When the chorus started, he slid his feet into a backwards glide. It made it look as though he was floating across the stage.

One slow step at a time, I crept toward Trey as I burst into my guitar solo. My fingers moved like lightning along the neck of my guitar.

Somebody in the back of the café whistled in appreciation. Almost everyone was bobbing their head to the pulsing beat. My beat. Trey might have been the one at the front of the stage, but the music was all my creation.

Spinning away from Trey, I finished the last two bars of my solo. I vibrated my finger on the strings and ended with a long, buzzing tremolo.

Harold hit both crash cymbals to finish the song.

Screams and whooping sounds came from every corner of the café. Many people got to their feet as they clapped. Behind the counter, the barista stuck her fingers into the sides of her mouth and let out a loud whistle.

I turned to the rest of the band, my heart pounding. Wasting no time, I stomped the foot switch on the stage to change the tone of my guitar to a gritty sound. Then I shouted the count-in to the next song as Harold clicked his drumsticks together four times.

I played the buttons on my groove pad like tiny finger drums. A melody of futuristic sounds, like something from outer space, came out of the speaker. Instantly, the crowd was hooked. Isaac added a bass groove that sent the crowd into a fever.

Our set finished with the final song, "Fiercely Independent." After we brought it to a big finish, we soaked up the long applause. Then we hustled to get our gear off the stage.

Gill Daring returned to the mic. "I think we just heard the next big sound to come out of the Showcase. Don't you?"

The crowd exploded into cheers.

Harold looked at me. "Can you believe this?"

Barely able to catch my breath, I shook my head. It didn't seem real.

On stage, Gill stuck his hand into the white bucket and pulled out a slip of paper. "Next up," he announced, "Electric Mermaid!"

We rushed away to give room for the next

band to set up their gear. I headed back to our table. As I passed the coffee counter, someone grabbed my arm from behind.

It was Gill Daring. "I'll need your phone number."

"Mine?" I was caught off guard.

He gave me another one of those blinding smiles. "You said this was your dream, right?"

"Totally."

"Then we should talk about things," Gill said.

"Things?"

"Big things," Gill said.

I tried to stop myself from smiling, but it wasn't easy. Still, I wanted to appear calm in front of Gill Daring. Serious. Like a pro.

I glanced at our table across the café. The others were watching me. Harold made a gesture with his hands, clearly asking me what was happening. All I could do was open my eyes wide with excitement.

I turned back to Gill and recited my number.

He tapped it into his phone. "I'll be in touch soon," Gill said. Then he snapped his fingers at the barista, a young woman behind the counter. "Kalli, honey. Get my new friend here an Italian soda. On the house. She must be thirsty."

New friend? Me?

After Gill headed back to his table, Kalli passed me a plastic cup of soda.

"Thanks," I said, taking a long sip.

Kalli shook her head. "Trust me, it won't be me you'll have to thank."

Her voice had a weird ring to it, like she was warning me not to look straight at the sun. Just as I was about to ask what she meant, a customer came to the counter and ordered a vanilla latte.

"Great set," the guy said to me. "You've got a future in music."

I smiled. The guy was right.

I *did* have a future in music.

All thanks to hundreds of hours of practice.

And Gill Daring.

Chapter 3

Sweet Dreams

"One hundred people have listened to 'Contagious' and 'Fiercely Independent' since our show!" I said.

Inside Spinners — my favourite used record store — I held my phone in front of Harold's face. On the screen was SoundCloud, the online site where we uploaded all our music. Before last week, only ten people had ever listened to our songs online. Mostly family and friends.

It was Wednesday after school and the store was empty. I was always on the search for old records to sample music from. I would record short clips of the lyrics or a small part of the beat. I got into soul music when I had heard my favourite rappers use samples of old soul songs in their music. It added a cool vibe to our rap rock sound. Aretha Franklin. Ray Charles. Al Green. Percy Sledge. There were so many great ones to choose from.

With my thumb I switched to Instagram while flipping through stacks of records. "I can't stop checking the Showcase's Instagram page," I said.

"Me neither," Harold said. He was flipping through the records next to me.

I scrolled through dozens of comments about our open mic set and read a few to Harold. "Listen to these new ones. Somebody said we're the next Linkin Park! Wicked guitarist . . . Sound design was amazing . . . Super original . . . Stellar vibe from Shadow Beat . . .

Tight band, can't wait to see them again . . .
Gill Daring was right: Shadow Beat is the next
big sound."

"Just in time," Harold said. "Yannick and
Isaac were close to quitting the band. Can't
really blame them. Until last Friday, we'd only
ever played three live shows." Harold started
to count on his fingers. "One, the Family Day
Festival. Out of all the stages, they stuck us on
the one near the pond with the mosquitoes.
Nobody came, remember? Two, the school
talent show. Total disaster. Half the gear didn't
work. Three, the Lilyflower Seniors' Centre —
an old folks' home. What rap rock band plays
at an old folks' home?"

"Good things take time, Harold. Every
overnight success was years in the making."
I rolled my eyes at myself. When did I start
quoting my mother?

I slid my phone back into the front of my
grey hoodie. Every day I wore jeans, baggie
concert T-shirts, cozy sweatshirts. Nothing like

what I wore on stage. I loved dressing like a different person when I performed. The person I was on stage was bold and confident and in control.

"Open Mic Night was the best thing ever," Harold said.

"I can't believe Gill Daring has my number," I said. "Did you know that Gill graduated only two years ahead of my brother? Jose told me that Gill was a superstar in high school. But nobody guessed he'd become such a big shot."

Harold looked like he suddenly remembered something. He checked the calendar on his phone. "I forgot we've got that sound check tomorrow after school."

Harold and I had volunteered to run the sound system for our high school's big production of *Grease*. I had even made sound effects for the car scenes. We worked behind the scenes, so nobody would know we were in the back corner of the gym working my magic.

Secretly, I wished my parents were home to see the play and hear all my hard work.

For the past six weeks, my parents had been on a business trip to Mexico. Again. They had been gone a lot over the last four years. Months at a time. I really missed having them around, especially since my brother, Jose, was hardly home from his job in the evenings. But my parents were following their dreams. Following your dreams was something I understood.

Harold pulled out an album and handed it to me. "Here it is!"

It was a Percy Sledge album from the 1960s called *The Percy Sledge Way*. I had been searching for it for months. Now I only needed his album *Warm and Tender Soul* to make my Percy Sledge collection complete.

As we stood at the cashier counter, Harold asked if we could stop by the Women's Crisis Centre where his mom worked. It was a place that supported women who had been assaulted or abused. It was just around the corner from the record store.

"All right," I said. "But I'll wait outside."

I had known Ms. Fox since I was ten, and I loved her like a second mom. But the Women's Crisis Centre freaked me out. You never saw any of the women in Ms. Fox's office because they needed privacy. Some needed protection if they were still in danger. The thought of seeing one of them with a bruised face or worse scared me. It was like another world I knew nothing about.

"After that, let's head over to the used record store on East 2nd," I suggested. "Maybe they have that last album for my collection."

"East 2nd?" Harold groaned. "I don't know. That's a bad part of town. My dad got mugged there once. It's all crime and hardcore druggies."

"Oh, come on. Nothing's going to happen to us."

Harold raised his eyebrows at me. "I know

you think you're invincible, Ana. But you know you're not, right?"

"Not invincible," I agreed. "Fiercely independent."

✷✷✷

As soon as I got home, I took a photo of my new album and posted it on my Instagram with the caption: *Great find today. Can't wait to sample the songs and chop up some new beats. Only need to hunt down the* Warm and Tender Soul *album to complete my collection. Impossible to find.*

After dinner, I worked on some new sounds. You could get all kinds of music samples and loops online for free, but I preferred to make my own from scratch. With my phone, I recorded the drip of the bathroom faucet and the clang of two cooking pots. Then I played the new album on my turntable, recording parts of it into my computer. I worked with the recorded clips on my computer, turning them into something I could use as a strange drum beat or a cool synthesizer.

The whole time I kept checking my social media. Our songs were up to two hundred listens. More than two hundred people now followed us on our band's Instagram page. My stomach swirled with excitement.

I slid on my headphones and opened my new sounds in my DAW — my digital audio workstation. I started to lay down some tracks. Sometimes it took me hours to get the sounds just right, but I loved it. It was like getting lost in another world where nothing mattered but the music.

I used the clang of the cooking pots as a drum fill, then grabbed my guitar to play some chords over top. The groove was perfect. I could hear another great song taking shape. Better yet, now I could see how a live audience would move to the drop I was building into the song. Nothing compared to the electrifying feeling I had had on the open mic stage. I wanted to feel it again.

It was Wednesday, so Jose wouldn't be getting home from his job until three o'clock in the morning. He was a bouncer at Changes Nightclub downtown. On nights like this, I usually crawled under the covers in my parents' bed and played one of my old Disney movies on their TV. It was my little secret. If anyone found out that fiercely independent Shadow Santos was scared to be alone at night, I would die.

Just as I climbed into my parents' bed, my phone buzzed. When I glanced at the screen, my mouth dropped.

It was Gill Daring.

We need to talk about your career.

I read his message about twenty times. I didn't know how to respond.

Finally I texted: When?

Come to the Showcase tomorrow afternoon at 3:30. Just you. Not the whole band. I want to talk about the sound design you do.

My heart raced. A meeting with Gill Daring. I texted back.

Got it. See you then.

I couldn't stay still. I tossed and turned on the bed as *The Lion King* played on the TV. Halfway through the movie I finally closed my eyes. I muttered something my dad said to me every night when he was home.

"Sweet dreams."

I smiled to myself.

My dreams *were* getting sweet.

Chapter 4

My Big Break

At school the next day, I wasn't able to concentrate on a thing. Not even Music class. All I could think about was my big meeting with Gill Daring. Then I was so freaked out about being late that I got to the Showcase a half hour early. I sat across the street in my pickup truck and tried to read my Biology text until it was time.

Inside, the place was nearly empty. A young woman sipped coffee in the corner. She looked up from whatever she was writing in her notebook and nodded at me. I smiled in return, but she kept the same serious look on her face. I pegged her to be a real snob, but then decided to cut her some slack. You never knew what crappy things a person might be facing each day.

At the counter, I found Kalli working again.

"I'm supposed to meet Mr. Daring at three thirty," I explained.

"Gill. He'll get mad if you call him Mr. Daring," Kalli said. Then she pointed across the café. "He's in his office. Through those doors past the stage."

"Thanks," I said.

Kalli spritzed the counter with cleaner. "You might want to leave the door open."

"All right," I said with a shrug.

As I walked past the stage, I stopped for a minute. The sight of the amps and mic stands brought it all back. The vibration of my guitar.

The lights. The heat. The crowd clapping and whistling.

Through the door was a long, dim hallway. Old concert posters lined the walls. Music played somewhere down the hall. I recognized it right away. Aretha Franklin. I had sampled that album and used it as the hook in a song I was working on. I headed down the hall, then turned a corner. Right in front of me was a second door. It was closed. I took a deep breath and knocked.

A voice called out from inside. "Come in."

Inside, Gill Daring sat behind a large desk. Along one wall of the small office was an old piano. Along the other wall was a large leather couch. The Aretha Franklin song played on the turntable in the corner.

Gill's face cracked into a wide smile when he saw me. "There she is! My next big star!" He threw down his pen and waved for me to enter the room.

I took a few steps into the office and nodded at the turntable. "You like Aretha Franklin?"

"Oh, I love soul music," he said.

"Really? I collect soul albums," I said.

"No way!" He clapped his hands together. "I collect them, too!"

"I use them as samples and vocal chops in my songs," I said. I could hardly believe that I was talking about music with Gill Daring. It was intimidating, that was for sure. But I managed to stay relaxed. "Best place for rare finds is the used store on East 2nd."

"I'll check it out. Thanks for the tip," Gill said. "Well, don't be shy. Come in! Let's see some of that confidence you show on stage! And close the door, would you?"

I clutched the doorknob, then stopped. I thought about what Kalli had said about leaving the door open.

"Noise from the café travels down the hall," Gill explained. "Better to have the door closed."

I closed the door and took a seat on the leather couch.

"Before business, first tell me how school was today," he said. "Must keep you busy. You do any extra stuff at school? Sports? Clubs?"

"Actually, I'm the sound engineer for our school's production of *Grease*. Designed all the special effects myself."

"When's the big show?" Gill picked up his pen.

"Next month," I said. "May fifteenth."

"Must be disappointing that your parents aren't here to see these things. Mexico, right?" Gill jotted something down on a piece of paper. He kept talking without waiting for me to answer. "Any other family who can watch your genius in action?"

Genius? I tried not to beam. "My brother, Jose. But he works almost every night. He's hardly ever free."

"Jose." Gill screwed up his face in concentration. "Jose Santos. Rings a bell. Did he also go to Central High?"

"He was two years behind you," I said. "He remembers you."

Gill snapped his fingers. "Yes, I remember now. Great guy."

"He is," I said proudly.

"Come over here. I want you to look at something." Gill handed me a thin stack of papers. "Your contract. Well, Shadow Beat's contract. But let's be real. Shadow Beat is nothing without you. You *are* Shadow Beat."

My cheeks went hot. I imagined them bright red, which made them grow even hotter. It was true that I wrote all the music and most of the lyrics. But I felt guilty hearing Gill leave the others out like that. Still, it was flattering.

Gill stroked the stubble on his jaw, which was sharp, like the kind on the cover of men's fashion magazines. "I'm offering Shadow Beat a regular slot on Friday nights. Ten o'clock."

I almost choked on my tongue. "Fridays? That's your busiest night."

"Busiest time slot, too." Gill pointed at the contract. "This is your chance to launch your career."

I took a deep breath. *Wait until the band hears about this*, I thought.

"You deserve this, Ana. Everyone loved your sound. Your songs are going to be smash hits. You're a natural on stage. You've got charisma. A commanding presence. It's rare to find talent combined with a perfect look."

Me? A perfect look? I had never thought of myself that way. Not even close. Sure, I'd had guys at school ask me out on dates and I'd had a couple of boyfriends. But I had only ever thought of myself as okay looking. Far from perfect. Then again, that was Ana Santos. Shadow Santos was sexy. Confident.

Gill held out a pen. "I'll need you to sign the contract today. Your first performance is tomorrow night."

"Tomorrow —?" I was surprised at the short notice, but I stopped myself. I wanted to appear ready. "Tomorrow night."

"As you'll see in the contract, the band gets paid one hundred and fifty dollars per night."

Paid? How amazing was that? Sure, it split up into only thirty dollars for each of us. But the idea that someone was even paying me to play my music thrilled me.

"It's the standard contract I give to all my regular bands," he said.

Taking the pen, I skimmed through the pages of the contract. I didn't understand what most of the legalese meant. Too excited to question any of it, I set the contract on the desk. At the bottom of the last page was a line. Underneath the line it read, *Shadow Beat*.

"You just need to sign on that line as a member of Shadow Beat," he said.

I wondered if I should talk to the rest of the band first. But what for? As if they would say no to a regular gig.

I signed my name.

Chapter 5

Friday Night Famous

"One, two, three, four!"

Harold called the count-in from behind the drum kit. We launched into "Contagious" in front of a packed café that Friday night. It was a completely different audience from the one at Open Mic Night. Those had been mostly other musicians.

I was wearing a short black dress with black stockings and my tall black boots. I still had some stage jitters. But mostly I was pumped.

The Friday night slot meant there were more couples out on dates. So the staff had moved the front tables to make a small dance floor. By the time we hit the second chorus of the song, ten or so people had gathered in front of the stage to dance. They were dancing to *my* music. I had created something that made people want to dance. Me.

It didn't hurt that Trey was dancing a lot more tonight. From the start, he sang with confidence as he swaggered around the stage. Many people in the audience were mesmerized by his voice and his moves.

But Trey didn't take the whole spotlight. People watched me, too. It was a little weird. I'd never had that kind of attention paid to me before. Trey loved being at the centre of things, but I just wanted to share my music. Sure, I loved to dress up as my alter ego, Shadow Santos. But all of it was about expressing myself. That, and feeling a magical connection with the crowd.

Like at Open Mic Night, as a band we were dialed in to one another. Our timing was perfect. The emotion in our playing was raw and powerful. Anyone could learn to move their fingers on the fretboard, but not everyone could play with emotion. At one point, Yannick burst into a keyboard solo during our song, "How Much Is Too Much?" It was unplanned, but the rest of us managed to groove with it. Harold followed with a killer solo on the drums. At the end of his solo, he hit the snare drum with both sticks. The sticks flipped high into the air, and he caught them on the way back down.

The crowd applauded loudly for both Yannick and Harold.

This time, we got to play more than three songs. Our set lasted half an hour, and the crowd loved all six songs. By the end, there were at least twenty-five people dancing wildly in front of the stage.

I shouted into the mic, "Let me see your hands in the air!"

Everyone on the dance floor raised their arms.

I was shocked. They actually did what I told them to. It was like I held them in the palm of my hand. It was a powerful feeling. Like nothing I'd ever felt before.

When we were packing up our gear after the show, dozens of people approached us. Three girls circled me and asked me to sign their napkins.

"You want *my* autograph?" I asked.

One of the girls nodded excitedly. "How long did it take you to learn to play guitar like that? Do you think I could learn?"

"Definitely," I said. I signed the napkin with both my stage name, Shadow, and my real name. "You can do anything you want."

"And those sounds you use on your groove pad," another girl said. "I read online that you make those yourself."

People were reading about me online? I grinned. "Of course I did. Only amateur music producers use stock sounds."

"I really want to get into music production," said the second girl. "I've been watching YouTube videos trying to learn. But there aren't a lot of female music producers."

"Guess we'll have to change that," I said.

The girl's face lit up. "You're like Rezz. You ever listen to her?"

"All the time." I really admired the Canadian musician.

"And WondaGurl," one of the other girls added.

Out of the corner of my eye, I saw a young woman tug down the neck of her T-shirt. She asked Trey to sign her bra with a black Sharpie. *Great*, I thought. *Just what the band needs. Something to make Trey's ego even bigger.*

"Now this is what I'm talking about!" Trey said to Yannick with a wiggle of his eyebrows. "We're Friday night famous!"

Yannick laughed. "That'd make a great song, 'Friday Night Famous.'"

I left the others to enjoy all the attention and headed to Gill's office. As I walked down the hall, I replayed my conversation with those girls. They looked up to me. Like I was somebody special.

"Ana!" Gill said when I walked into the office.

"Am I interrupting your work?" I asked.

Gill winked at me. "You can interrupt me anytime."

"I just wanted to thank you again for the chance you've given us."

"No, thank you. You sounded fantastic tonight. You commanded the stage with so much confidence again. You've got a fierce presence. And your moves — they're incredible. Mesmerizing."

Moves? How exactly did I move? I pictured myself on the stage. My fingers flying up and down the neck of my guitar. That was the only image that popped into my mind.

"I've got a few tips, if you want," Gill said. He leaned back and locked his fingers behind his head. "Just little things I've picked up from being in the business. My own special secrets for success."

"I'd love that," I said. I realized I was staring at the muscles bulging out of his T-shirt sleeves. He obviously worked out. I looked at the desk instead. "Anything to help me get ahead in the business."

"Now here's the only thing." He held up his hand. "If I help you, you have to keep this stuff to yourself. Don't want my trade secrets getting out."

I pretended to zip up my lips. "You have my word."

"Now and then someone with your talent comes through the Showcase's doors. Someone I choose to coach. But only if you're serious about your career."

"I am!" I said, louder than I meant to.

"Excellent. The first thing I want you to start thinking about is putting yourself front and centre of this band. You are Shadow, after all, and it is Shadow Beat. Trey's great, but he doesn't compare to you. Write some songs that you can sing lead on."

"We do have a couple that I sing," I said.

"Start performing them. And write more like that. We need to make it clear to the audience that you're the star here."

I winced. Trey wasn't going to like this.

"I know this business inside out," he said. "It's not often that I offer to coach someone. Only special cases."

Special cases. I was so excited I thought my chest was going to burst. Crossing my arms to hold it all in, I felt special standing there in his office.

Very special. Once-in-a-lifetime special.

Chapter 6

A Secret Gift

The next afternoon, I took my music gear over to Harold's house. Trey, Yannick and Isaac had soccer practice, so a full rehearsal would have to wait. In Harold's basement, I plugged in my guitar while he practised some basic drum patterns to warm up.

He finished a rhythm paradiddle across the toms. "Can't wait for my birthday. Finally get rid of this old drum set."

I ran through a few scales on my guitar.

"New drums? Nice!"

"My dad was thrilled about our weekly gig at the Showcase. I didn't think he even knew who Gill Daring was." Harold laughed. "But he says Gill is a big part of the community. It's the way he's turned the Showcase into a local launching pad for new talent." Harold played triplets lightly on the hi-hat. "Anyway, my dad was so proud he said I deserve a better drum set. The new Yamaha Studio edition."

"The metallic-red one you've been drooling over?"

Harold gazed up at the ceiling with a faraway look in his eyes. Since we first met in grade five, Harold was always a wild daydreamer. Just like me. It was one of the things that made us such good friends.

"Yep, the metallic-red one," he said, still gazing at the ceiling. "I have to kick in half the cost. Going to use some of the money from my summer house-painting job."

I let out a long whistle as I practised power chords.

Harold twirled his drumsticks. "Let's get started on that new groove."

"I was thinking something strong on the offbeat," I suggested. "Give it a funk vibe."

"Something like this?" Harold tested a few different beats.

"Try adding a little reggae flavour," I said.

"With a drop one?" Harold changed the rhythm by leaving off the "one" beat.

"That's it." I bobbed my head to the groove, then played a chord progression on my guitar. After a few bars, I said, "We'll get Isaac to play the bass part so that it emphasizes the kick drum. And then we'll layer in this —" I tapped the buttons on my groove pad. A dark-sounding synthesizer pattern played from speaker.

Harold's mouth dropped. "That is so good, Ana!"

I smiled with pride. "I made this synth sound by recording our kitchen blender at different speeds. Then I pitched the sounds down a few octaves. Added some filters."

"We're going to be big. I really believe it," Harold said.

"We're already up to three hundred followers on SoundCloud," I said. "And that's just the start. Wait until we've done a few more gigs. There's nothing to stop us, especially now that we have a contract!"

Harold dropped his sticks onto the snare with a rattle. "Wait. We have a contract? Since when do we have a contract?"

I wanted to kick myself. I tried to think up an excuse fast. But nothing came to me. I should have known that signing the contract without showing the others would come back to bite me.

"It's no big deal," I said, though I knew that wasn't true. If Trey or Isaac had signed a contract without talking to me, I would have been furious. Still, I downplayed it. "It was just the standard contract he gives all the regular bands."

"But how come he talked to you about it? Why weren't we there?"

I shrugged and left it at that. I was aching to tell Harold the exciting part about Gill offering to coach me in the music business. But the last thing I wanted was to make him feel left out.

"Can I at least see the contract?" Harold asked.

"Gill has it in his office."

"You didn't get a copy? I'm pretty sure you're supposed to get one," Harold said. "You better ask him for our copy before you sign it."

As I stared at the tiles on the floor, I figured it was only a matter of time before Harold found out. So, like ripping off a bandage, I got it over with.

"I've already signed it," I said.

At first Harold looked stunned. Then he inhaled a long breath through his nose. That's what he did when he was mad at me. "Why do you always have to do this? Act like you can handle everything on your own?"

Harold's words stung. But I dug in my heels. "I signed a contract for our band to get a great gig. Don't you think I'm smart enough to make sure we got a good deal?"

Harold relaxed his shoulders. "Fine. So what's the deal, then?"

"We get to play the ten o'clock slot every Friday. And we get paid one hundred and fifty dollars."

"Do we keep all the rights to our songs?" Harold asked.

"What do you mean?"

"Our songs will still belong to us, right?"

My stomach sunk. "I don't know."

"You don't know? Didn't it say in the contract?"

"I —" I hesitated. "I didn't read it."

Harold smacked his forehead. "You signed without reading it?"

"I was just so excited," I admitted. Why hadn't I read it more closely? When my mom and dad got their first business contract, they spent days reading every page. They even paid lawyers to read it. "Gill needed it signed right away because he wanted us to perform the next night."

Harold snapped his fingers. "Wait a second. You're under eighteen. I don't know if a minor can legally sign a contract."

I frowned. Why did Harold act like that was a good thing? If I was too young to sign a contract, there was no Friday night deal. "Are you sure? How come you know all this?"

"I told you to take Law Twelve this year. It's a great class. Lots of juicy crime stories." Harold grabbed his phone from the music stand and searched for something. After several minutes, he read the information he found. "In some cases a minor can sign a contract, in some cases you can't. The good news is that if there's something in it that's not right for the band, you can void it. Which means the contract can end. Just like that. There's an article here about Lil Pump. He was only seventeen when he signed a music contract with one of the big record companies. He was able to end it without getting into trouble."

"Will we lose our gig?" I asked.

"I don't think so," Harold said. "I'm sure the contract is fine. We're talking about Gill Daring here. I doubt he got this successful if he was a crook or anything."

✷✷✷

That night I got a text from Jose during his break at work. It was going to be another late night of work for him. But he was going to bring home my favourite chicken wings — Thai chili — from the restaurant next to the nightclub.

I was putting some reverb on a guitar track when my phone buzzed again. This time it was Gill.

Found something for you, he texted.

Then he sent a photo. It was the Percy Sledge album I had been looking for, *Warm and Tender Soul.*

For me? Was he giving me the album?

I'll leave it on your doorstep tomorrow. Wicks Street, right?

Yes, I texted. Awesome, thnx!

Don't tell anyone about it, k? Don't want collectors knowing I have a stash of albums. They'd never leave me alone. LOL.

When Gill had offered to coach me, I thought I couldn't feel any more special. But here I was, getting the collector's album I wanted. And yes, I could keep it a secret. I texted him my promise to not tell anyone. After all, what could be more flattering than to share a secret with none other than Gill Daring?

Chapter 7

A False Accusation

After school on Monday, I pulled my pickup into my driveway. It was a rusty thing with an old radio that crackled. I got it for a low price with the money I earned picking grapes at Wildrose Vineyards the summer before. Someday the band would have gigs all around town. Then my truck would be perfect for carrying amps and keyboards and drums.

On the wicker chair next to our front door was the album. The record cover was red and it had a picture of Percy Sledge singing on the front. I had a great idea for a downtempo rap song and I needed to sample the chorus of a song called "Try a Little Tenderness." Finding the song on YouTube or Spotify wasn't the same. I loved the authentic lo-fi sound of a vinyl record.

I stepped quietly through the house so I didn't wake Jose. He slept most of the day when he worked late. In my bedroom, I put the record on my turntable and thought about sending Gill another text to say thank you. It was thoughtful and kind of him to give me such a rare album.

First, I checked the band's Instagram. Then our SoundCloud listens, my own Instagram and finally the Showcase's Facebook page. I had been keeping a constant watch on the places where people were talking about Shadow Beat. It had been exciting to find new comments and check the number of new listeners, which was now up to four hundred.

But what I saw online shocked me.

The last post from the staff on the Showcase's Facebook page was a picture of the band Electric Mermaid. The caption reminded people that the Showcase was now serving gluten-free sandwiches. Underneath, was a comment that I couldn't figure out. Someone named Melissa Smith had typed a reply to the post.

Reminder: The Showcase now serves gluten-free sandwiches and unwanted touches from Gill Daring.

There was no profile pic of Melissa Smith, just a blank avatar and her comment.

I couldn't look away from the words "unwanted touches." My gaze was locked there. I turned my attention to the comments below Melissa Smith's statement. They made me sick to my stomach. But I couldn't tell whether I was worried or angry. Worried about what? And who was I angry at? Melissa Smith? For making a false accusation about Gill?

I wasn't the only angry one. Some comments attacked Melissa Smith. Others stood up for Gill Daring. Either way, one thing was clear. Gill Daring was being blamed for something he didn't do.

The more I read, the meaner the comments got:

Lying bitch.

Not true. Gill is a gentleman.

Haters gonna hate. You probably just suck at music, Melissa. Take your bitterness somewhere else.

Gill is the man!

The photo in the tiny circle next to this comment caught my eye. I zoomed in on the name. Trey Habermas.

I kept reading the comments from others:

Women should go to jail for lying about this shit.

She's fat and ugly, I bet.

You need a good smack to the face, Melissa Smith!

She needs some hot sex. HMU, Melissa! LOL

What a coward — an avatar for your pic?
Show us your face, Melissa!

I want to kill bitches like you.

Yeah, do us all a favour. Go and die.

Only one comment showed support for Melissa. It said: *#MeToo*. That was it. The name was Lyla Jones, and there was no photo. Both Melissa Smith and Lyla Jones were probably fake accounts. If these women didn't use their real names, how could anyone believe what they were saying?

Even so, it was one thing to be upset with this woman, but to want her dead? That seemed over the top. Some people liked to say extreme things online behind the comfort of their keyboard. The real question was: Why would anybody say this about Gill? Was she trying to blackmail him with lies?

I looked at the record on my turntable. It had to be blackmail. Or bitter revenge over something. Gill Daring was too nice to do stuff like that. Unwanted touches? He had been a total gentleman to me. And he supported me. Hell, he was taking the time to coach me. I wished the boys at my high school were more like Gill.

Picturing his big smile made me smile, too. No way did I have a thing for Gill. My mom would kill me if I ever dated a guy that age. But my mom had no reason to worry. Gill was two years older than my brother, too old for me. As if I'd ever have a chance with someone like him anyway. No, it wasn't like that at all. But there was something about him, I couldn't deny that. He was a magnet. A magnet who could open doors to my music career.

My mind seethed with thoughts until I didn't want to think about it anymore. I set the needle on my new record and listened to my secret gift before packing up for rehearsal at Harold's house.

✱✱✱

"I came up with a wicked song idea," I told the band during our first rehearsal break. "I recorded some sounds from my new Percy Sledge *Warm and Tender Soul* album. Too bad we can't use it, since we don't have permission to sample the song. But it might spark some new ideas for us."

"*Warm and Tender Soul?*" Harold gave me a confused look. "You finally found that album? When? Where? We looked in every record store."

Damn it. Why did I go and say that?

Turning to Harold, I smacked myself across the forehead for dramatic effect. "Did I say *Warm and Tender Soul?* I meant, *The Percy Sledge Way* — the one you found for me. Don't I wish I'd found *Warm and Tender Soul?!*" My laugh sounded super fake. Right away, I regretted lying to my best friend.

"You guys see that Facebook comment last night?" Trey asked.

"On the Showcase page? Yeah, I saw it," Yannick said. "What a liar."

"Internet makes it too easy for girls to lie about that shit," Trey agreed.

"They just do it for attention." Isaac took a swig of water from his bottle.

I tried not to be insulted by what they were saying about girls. I knew that Gill was the innocent victim here. But it didn't mean that I agreed with them. All girls didn't go around lying just for attention. Was that what they really thought?

"I don't know," Harold said. "According to my mom's research, very few women make false allegations."

"No way." Trey shook his head. "It happens a lot."

Harold shrugged. Trey had a stubborn streak. Sometimes there was no point in arguing with him. It got you nowhere.

"Good thing they pulled down the whole post last night," Isaac said. "It could ruin the guy's reputation."

Chapter 8

A Small Favour

The crowd at the Showcase was even larger the next Friday. All the tables were filled and people who couldn't find seats stood along the walls. I asked the sound and light technician, a guy named Tal, if he could turn on the fog machine at the start of our first song, "Neon Mist."

"Did you run it by Gill?" Tal wriggled his wool cap onto his head.

I hesitated. There was no time to talk to Gill.

But the fog machine would create the perfect atmosphere for that song. The idea had come to me the night before as I drifted off to sleep. In my mind, it would look mysterious. Almost mystical.

"Of course, she ran it by me," said a voice from behind me. It was Gill. He picked up the fog machine and an extra set of mood lights. "In fact, I offered to help set it up for her."

As Gill headed to the stage, Tal pushed his cap back. "Wow, not sure what you said to him. In the five years I've worked here, I have never seen Gill Daring lift a single thing."

At precisely ten o'clock, Shadow Beat waited on the darkened stage. As the fog filled the air around us and the red lights shone down on me, people whistled and hollered with excitement. This crowd was ready to party.

A few days earlier, I had gone shopping at the thrift store and found a black motorcycle jacket made of fake leather. Tonight I wore it over a black tank top with lace trim. My black jeans had large rips in the thighs that showed my skin. The whole outfit made me feel like a rebel.

I started the song's intro with a slow, crunchy guitar riff. The others waited in the shadows for their cue to join in. The fog machine created the exact effect I had imagined.

I scanned the café for Gill. I hoped he thought the fog machine was worth the effort. I spotted him behind the coffee counter. He had his arm wrapped around Kalli's shoulders. Only an innocent man would dare do that after being accused of unwanted touches. Maybe he didn't know about Melissa Smith's comment. Gill tilted his head toward Kalli and laughed.

I felt a tightness in my chest as I watched Gill pull Kalli close to him. It seemed friendly, but was it more than that? Was I really going to get jealous? I inwardly laughed at myself. That wasn't my style. I was too focused on my music to waste energy on negative feelings. I thought again about Melissa Smith's comment on Facebook. Gill was just one of those guys who was friends with everyone. That's all there was to it.

The whole night went great, except for something that happened at the end. After we had finished talking to people from the crowd, Trey pulled me aside.

"You called 'Contagious' *our* song," he said.

"It is our song," I said.

Trey poked at his chest. "I wrote the lyrics."

"So?" I put my hands on my hips. "I wrote the guitar riff, the bass line and the keyboard chords. Harold came up with the beat. Plus, I created all the risers and synth stabs."

"But the lyrics are what make the song stick in people's heads," Trey argued. "It's the most important part."

"Says you."

"We should make an agreement about

who owns our songs. Put something in writing. Before things take off for us."

I narrowed my eyes at Trey. Where was this coming from all of a sudden? Trey had never cared about this stuff before. But it did remind me of Harold's question about our contract. One time, I had seen a documentary about Motown musicians whose songs were stolen by a crooked producer.

Maybe Trey had a point.

At least he hadn't brought up the contract. That meant that Harold hadn't told the others about it. As long as they got paid, I hoped they would have no reason to think there even was a contract.

✳ ✳ ✳

In Biology class on Monday, my phone buzzed. Ms. Semple was just wrapping up her lecture on cellular respiration. Last class of the day. Although I had managed to take down the notes, I was thinking of ideas for our next show.

Like the album?

It was Gill.

Love it. ty!

Great to complete a collection, Gill texted. Only us collectors understand.

I smiled and texted, Totally.

Suddenly I realized that I was the only one left in the classroom. Even Ms. Semple was gone. I closed my Biology text and grabbed my backpack from between my feet. I packed everything away except my phone. I looked at the screen. Gill had sent another text.

Wondering if I could ask you for a small favour.

I didn't hesitate. Sure!

Before hitting SEND, I deleted the exclamation mark.

Could you meet me at the Showcase tomorrow with your truck? Our van broke down and I have to make an important delivery.

Tomorrow? The band had a big rehearsal planned. Trey was bringing his new lyrics and we were going work on the music.

What time? I asked.

Five sharp.

Rehearsal was at six. Maybe I could squeeze both in.

Okay, see you then, I replied.

How long could a delivery take? Not long, I hoped. The guys would be pretty upset with me if I was late. It was one of the rules we made when we first started Shadow Beat. Never keep the rest of the band waiting.

Chapter 9

A Good Guy

Gill was out front when I pulled up at the Showcase. On the sidewalk beside him was a row of trays covered with aluminum foil. As I hopped out, Gill was loading the first tray onto the bed of my pickup. He motioned for me to grab one of the others.

"Sandwiches," Gill explained as I slid the tray next to his. "They're a day old. Still perfectly good, but we can't sell them now."

What a relief. A delivery of four sandwich

trays shouldn't take long. I'd be setting up my music gear at Harold's with plenty of time to spare. I'm not even sure why he needed my truck. Four trays could easily fit inside the trunk of a car. After the last tray was loaded, I started to lift the tailgate. But Gill put his hand on it and stopped me.

"We have to get the other food first," he said.

For the next twenty minutes, I followed Gill up and down both sides of the block. From each café and coffee shop we collected sandwiches, doughnuts, pastries and bagels. In every place we went, people acted like Gill was the sun after a stormy day. Their faces lit up to see him. It felt pretty good to be seen with someone like that.

By the time we finished, the back of my truck was stacked with food. I checked the time on my phone. Quarter to six. My stomach turned. How did it get so late? If the delivery was quick, maybe I could still make it to rehearsal on time.

"Head down to East 2nd," Gill said as he closed the passenger door.

East 2nd? That would take twenty minutes in traffic. I was losing hope quickly. When we finally reached the downtown area, I checked my phone again. Ten after six. I was doomed.

"Need to be somewhere?" Gill asked.

"Uh — yeah, rehearsal," I said. "At six."

"Oh," he said. His voice sounded sorry. He pointed at the abandoned lot he wanted me to pull in to. "I doubt you'll make any of it. Not by the time we hand all these out."

I took it slow over the potholes so the food wouldn't flip out of the truck. Past a crumbling wall of concrete was a group of homeless people.

"Take a tray and head that way," Gill said. "I'll go over there. Let them choose what they want. It helps them keep their dignity."

"I should text the guys first," I said.

Gill shook his head. "Some of these people haven't eaten for days. What's worse?

Making the guys wait a little longer? Or —" he motioned to the homeless people — "making *them* wait for food?"

Leaving my phone in my pocket, I walked a tray over to some men sitting on the ground against a wall. My nerves were on edge. I didn't know what I was supposed to say to them. The guy at the end shooting drugs into his arm hardly filled me with confidence. But I figured if Gill had done this before, then it must be safe.

It took just a few minutes to unload all the food off one tray. As I headed back to the pickup to grab another tray, I heard Gill's voice around the corner.

"Quit wasting my time, old man. Just take a damn sandwich," Gill said.

I peeked around the wall. Gill was alone with a homeless man.

"Thank you," said the homeless man. "God bless you, sir. You're a kind soul."

Gill sneered. "Have some pride, old man. You sound pathetic."

I tried to make sense of what I was hearing. Gill's words were sharp. Mean. Nothing like the Gill who had collected the food from shops on the street. Greeting everybody with a friendly smile.

By the time we were done with all the trays, it was almost eight. When I looked at my phone, it was worse than I expected. I had eighteen texts from the guys asking where the hell I was.

"The band?" Gill glanced at my phone as we climbed back into the truck.

I nodded. I couldn't shake the feeling that I'd let them down. Then again, I just helped Gill Daring do something kind for other people. Not to mention how good it felt to do a favour for him. After what he had done for us. For me.

"Would it help if you told them you got the band an interview with Winder Media?" Gill asked. "Their articles appear in all kinds of newspapers and online outlets. You'll get amazing exposure."

"We have an interview?"

Gill nodded at my phone. "Tell them that's why you didn't make it. You were stuck on the phone with the media people. Interview is tomorrow."

"For real?" I asked.

"Would I lie?"

I let out the breath I'd been holding. Maybe the guys wouldn't be mad after all. Not once they heard that Shadow Beat had its first interview.

Gill must have seen the relief on my face. "Better?"

"Yeah," I said.

"We're friends now," he said. "I scratch your back. You scratch mine."

✳✳✳

"How do I look?" Harold asked me outside the Showcase.

"Like a star," I said.

Trey, Yannick and Isaac came around the corner together.

"You guys ready for Shadow Beat's first interview?" I asked.

"First of many." Trey winked.

I flung open the front door and glanced at Kalli behind the counter. Kalli motioned her head toward a table where a woman sat.

"Hello," the woman said when we approached. "Samantha Thanh."

As I sat down, I wiped my sweaty palms on my jeans and took a deep breath. I'd never been interviewed before.

Once Samantha had written down our names, she jumped right into her questions. "When did Shadow Beat come together as a band?"

"Two years ago," I replied. "We were in grade ten. I'd been creating beats on my computer and playing guitar with Harold for a year or so. One day we decided to make a band. So I put up some flyers on the bulletin board at our high school. That's how Trey, Yannick and Isaac joined."

"Who is the creative heart of the group?" Samantha asked.

"I wrote the lyrics for 'Contagious,'" Trey said. "It's probably our biggest hit."

"But Ana writes most of the songs," Harold said. "The lyrics and the music."

Samantha nodded. "You combine electronic music production with your own brand of rock rap. It's a pretty unique sound. Who came up with it?"

"That was all Ana," Harold said.

"Not *all* Ana," Trey sneered.

Samantha ignored Trey. "How did you land the Friday night gig here at the Showcase?"

Yannick pumped his fist in the air. "We rocked Open Mic Night! Next thing we knew, we had a gig."

"Thanks to Gill Daring," Trey said.

"Will you credit Gill Daring, then, if you

become successful?" Samantha asked.

"Sure," said Trey. "But there's no success without us."

"True," Samantha said. "But the music industry is very tough. YouTube, SoundCloud, Spotify — online places make it easier to break into the business yourself. But it's still hard to do. Gill Daring can make or break a band's local career."

"If the band has talent," Trey persisted.

"So would you say it's an even trade? His connections and influence for your talent and creativity?" Samantha narrowed her eyes thoughtfully.

"I'd say that," Isaac said.

Samantha leaned forward. "Does Gill expect you to trade more than your talent and creativity?"

Trey laughed. "What's more than our talent and creativity?"

Samantha looked straight at me. "The music industry is full of rumours. About the kinds of deals that are made. The deals that aren't put in writing. The stuff people don't talk about but everyone knows about. The open secrets."

"No secrets here," Trey said. "Just raw talent. Plain and simple."

"Do you really think it's that simple?" Samantha raised an eyebrow.

Trey gave a firm nod. "It's that simple."

I wanted to groan. What did Trey know about it? I did all the work for the band. Running the social media accounts. Recording, mixing and mastering the songs to put online. Composing most of the music.

"I agree. It's that simple. We rock the crowd, we get paid," Isaac said.

"Do you think success will put a strain on the relationships between band members?" Samantha asked.

"Never," Yannick said. "We're tight."

I tried to not look surprised by his answer. Tight? Last month Yannick and Isaac were ready to quit the band.

"The demands to put out new music, the swarms of fans, the hectic performance schedule," Samantha said. "It can take a toll. I've seen it many times. Band members start to get jealous about the attention others are getting."

"Not us," Trey said.

When the interview was over, Samantha got the band to pose for a picture. Then she handed me a business card. "If you think of anything else I should know — *anything* — just call or text me."

Just then, Gill came in the front door. He pointed at the band and said, "Just the people I wanted to see. We need to discuss your songs."

"What about them?" Trey asked.

"You've played the same songs three weeks in a row," Gill said.

"People love our songs," Trey said.

"Yes, but they expect fresh material. *I* expect fresh material."

"We don't have any new songs ready yet," Harold said.

I covered a smile with my hand. Harold was painfully honest at times.

"Then you better get to work," Gill said.

"Don't worry," Trey said. "I've got some new stuff that will blow you away. We'll start rehearsing the fresh material this week."

"And I want to see more variety in who sings lead," Gill said.

"What?" Trey's face went bright red.

Gill explained, "Make sure some of these new songs are sung by Ana."

Trey turned and glared at me, as if I had put Gill up to this.

"New songs, and Ana sings more," Gill said. "Or you lose your spot."

Chapter 10
#MeToo

Hunching over my groove pad, I plugged the cables into the speaker on stage. We had ten minutes before our set started. I felt a hand touch my back. I turned to see Gill. He took a step back and looked me over from head to toe.

"Love what you're wearing tonight. You look like a real rock star."

I wore a black jean jacket and a pair of black cargo pants. The cargo pants were much too big for me. But that's what I liked about them.

They gave me a hip hop feel I was going for that night. The pants hung low on my hips. So, with my cropped black T-shirt, the lower half of my stomach was bare. I was hoping the stage lights would glint off the fake diamond in my belly ring.

"I've been thinking," Gill said. "We should probably get some promotional pictures done."

"Sounds great," I said. "I'll let the band know."

Gill shook his head. "Not the band. Just you."

I wilted at the idea. It seemed like a betrayal to the band. Like I was going behind their backs. After being late for rehearsal and Gill's request that I sing more, I didn't want to piss them off again.

Gill tilted his head to one side. "If you're worried about the others, don't. They'll never know about this. Or at least, by the time they do, it won't matter."

It won't matter? What did that mean? If I

didn't know better, Gill was making it sound as though Shadow Beat's days were numbered.

"It's just —" I had to say something. "We're a band. I'd feel shitty to ditch them like that. Especially Harold."

"I understand," Gill said. "But I told you. You're my next big star. And I know it's hard to think about now. But all stars have to leave some people behind."

I looked around the place. The crowd had been getting coffee and chatting at their tables since the earlier band had finished their set.

"I've contacted my photographer and a makeup artist. I'm doing a lot for you here. All I need is for you to realize that the rest of Shadow Beat —" He took a deep breath. "Ana, they're going to hold you back. You told me you were ready to do anything for your dream. Remember?"

"I remember."

Gill hopped off the stage, leaving me in a daze. The thought of sneaking behind everyone's back worried me. Then again, what if Gill was right? What if Shadow Beat was holding me back?

The first half of our show went smoothly. The crowd was less energetic than the audience the previous week. But we gave a good performance. The closer we got to the end of our show, the more I dreaded the idea of betraying the band. Neither choice was good. Go behind the guys' backs and make Gill happy. Or say no to Gill and risk losing all this. If I was honest with myself, I wasn't at all torn between the two choices. Because I *was* ready to do whatever it took to launch my music career. The only thing I felt bad about was that I didn't feel bad enough.

I had no clue what Gill planned to use the photos for. But I trusted him. He knew what he was doing. I only needed to look at all the successful musicians on the walls to know that.

The whole thing must have bugged me more than I thought. During our second to last song, I started my part of the chorus late. It threw the band's timing off. The crowd didn't notice, but Trey glared at me.

Things got worse during our final song, "Free Heart." Besides "Fiercely Independent," it was one I was most proud of writing, with its message of being yourself. It was also one of the few songs I sang lead on.

As I belted out the first verse, my voice felt shaky. The band burst into the chorus with Trey singing background vocals. I stumbled over a few words. Trey gave me another look, this time more of a question than a glare.

By the time we reached the third verse, I was thrown off by my mistakes. It's the mark of a good musician to recover from stumbles, but I wasn't able to get back on track. I started to worry about my performance, which made me tense up even more. My voice got tight, too. I strained to finish a line of lyrics without taking an extra breath.

Again, Trey glared at me and pointed his finger at his temple.

I got his point. *Concentrate.*

We finished the last chorus, then the short ending. Compared to the applause after our earlier songs, the crowd's response to my vocals was low key. I wanted to get home as soon as possible. I needed to crawl into my parents' bed and put tonight behind me.

After our set, I unplugged all my gear and hurried to the back corner where I kept my guitar case. The rest of the band was busy chatting with fans at the front of the stage. It gave me a chance to slip away without any of them asking about my poor performance.

When I closed my guitar case, I saw that someone had put a sticker on it during our show. It was rectangular, about the size of my palm. In big block letters it read:

#METOO

***

I sat at the desk in my bedroom and stared at my guitar case. Who would vandalize my stuff like that? I tried to peel off the sticker, but it tore and left a sticky mess.

I fired up my computer and searched *#MeToo* on the Internet. I had seen the hashtag on Facebook and Twitter. I knew it had something to do with sexual abuse, like in the movie industry.

As I expected, most of the search results led to individual Twitter accounts. But there were also links to newspaper articles and blogs. From what I was reading, the *#MeToo* hashtag was started by a woman named Tarana Burke. The idea was to break the silence. That women who had been harassed or assaulted could speak out about it online. Many famous actors had spoken out, saying that they'd been harassed or assaulted by powerful men as part of their careers in show business.

I kept coming across the phrase "casting couch." It was a way of referring to how a powerful person, usually a man, demanded sex from actors in exchange for an acting job. The actor would be cast in the movie or TV show only if they got on the couch and had sex.

I glanced again at the sticker on my case. People put stickers all the time on road signs and on the walls outside fast-food drive-thrus. It must have been something like that. Somebody trying to get the word out by plastering stickers everywhere they went. Just a fluke that it ended up on my guitar case.

Because this had nothing to do with me.

Chapter 11

A New Promise

On Saturday, I packed the truck with my music gear. After the performance the night before I didn't feel like rehearsing. But I couldn't bail on the guys again. Besides, I was dying to hear Trey's new songs. The guy could be stubborn and full of himself, but he had a way with lyrics. There was no denying that. As I backed out of the driveway, my phone dinged with a text.

Showcase in a half hour. Big news.

In a half hour? No, I couldn't. Of course, I didn't want to say no to Gill. But I'd have to lie to the band again. I couldn't let them know I was meeting Gill on my own. Not after Harold asked me why I was the only one to meet with Gill about the contract. Good thing they were all too excited about the interview to ask how I got it for us.

I texted Harold. Gonna be late.

He answered right away. Again? How late?

Not sure. Sorry.

What's up with you? Harold texted.

Tell you later, I lied.

I felt hollow inside. Before all this started, I had only ever lied to Harold once. We were twelve and I stole his last cookie when he left the room. I said his dog ate it. Now I'd lied to him twice in a week. First about the Percy Sledge album. Then about what I was doing the night I missed rehearsal. If I kept this up, my lies would build a wall between me and Harold.

I turned off my phone.

***

The moment I entered Gill's office, he got straight to the point.

"I got you two slots at the Endless Summer Festival," he said.

My mouth opened in surprise. Endless Summer Festival was a week-long music event held in Holland Park next to the mall. It attracted huge crowds and media. I'd heard that more than a hundred bands apply each year for a time slot.

"On the big stage," he added.

My heart fluttered into my throat. I was speechless.

"Shadow Beat will have a slot. And you will have a solo slot."

I'd never performed on my own. A solo gig scared me, but I didn't let on.

"That's why we need to get your photos

done. Promotional posters advertising the Shadow Santos concert. For the next two months, expect to see your face all over town."

✳✳✳

I finally made it to rehearsal at Harold's house. Not quite an hour late. At least Gill had given me more amazing news to tell the band. If I didn't have that, they probably would have locked me out of the basement. Of course I didn't dare tell them about my solo spot at the festival. Trey would have a fit. And I didn't want Harold to think that I was moving on without him. Though that's exactly what seemed to be happening.

"Look, I'm really sorry guys," I said. "But I've got big news. We've been given a spot at the Endless Summer Festival!"

"No way!" Isaac smacked both his cheeks.

"Oh, man," Yannick said. "This is huge!"

"How did that happen?" Harold asked.

He sounded excited, but I could hear something else in his voice. He was suspicious of me.

"Now's the perfect time to check out my new songs." Trey rummaged through his backpack and pulled out pieces of crumpled paper. He waved them in the air. "Three new kick-ass songs for the festival!"

"Pass them around," Isaac said.

Shaking his head, Trey stood up. "I'm going to sing them for you. That way you can hear just how great they are."

"Sounds good to me," Yannick said. "What do you want us to play?"

Trey shuffled through the papers. "Let's do this one first. It's called 'Get Down on This.' It's in the key of D. So, Yannick, do a basic chord progression on the keyboards. Harold, give me something with a hip hop vibe. But with a snare on three."

Harold started to play. Then he turned his stick around and played the snare on the rim, making a clicking sound.

"That's it." Trey started moving his body to the beat. He looked down at the paper and rapped the first verse.

I winced as I listened. The vibe was good and Trey's rhymes were on fire. There was only one problem. The lyrics.

"That song is great!" Isaac said.

"Smoking-hot rhymes," Yannick agreed.

Trey turned to me. "Ana, layer your signature sounds over this and we've got a hit. What do you think?"

"I can't play this song," I said.

Trey pushed his cap back. "You'll find the sounds for it. You always do."

"No," I said. "I mean I *won't* play this song."

"You won't play it?" Isaac asked.

"Why not? It's awesome," Yannick said.

"The song is basically saying that women are good for one thing. Sex," I said. "Specifically oral sex. You're ordering them to 'Get Down on This.'"

Yannick laughed. "Is that what it's about?"

"You know it is," I said.

Trey shrugged. "Yeah, but this is the kind of stuff that goes viral."

"It's not the only stuff that goes viral." I took the papers from Trey. "Let me see these. Maybe we can focus on one of the other songs."

After skimming Trey's lyrics, I slapped the papers against my leg in frustration. I handed the song sheets to Yannick, who read them and then passed them along.

"All these lyrics are so demeaning to women," I said.

Trey flapped his hand at me. "Quit being so sensitive."

"Yeah, Ana," Isaac said. "These songs are too good to ignore."

Harold sat at his drum set reading through the lyrics. "Ana's right. These lyrics will make us sounds like pigs."

"But they're so good!" Yannick said.

"What if we change some of the really bad lyrics but keep the same vibe," Harold suggested. "Make a compromise."

"No way," Trey said. "I'm not compromising my artistic vision."

"I agree with Trey," Isaac said. "Why should he have to change anything?"

"Why should I have to play these songs?" I took the sheets back from Harold. "Right here, for example. 'Girl, don't bother with that talking, you know that's not what your mouth is for.'"

Isaac snickered.

"You think that's funny?" I glared at Isaac, then turned to Trey. "Artistic vision? It's your artistic vision that I'm just a piece of meat to be used however you want?"

"The songs aren't about you," Trey protested.

"They're about females," I said. "Last I checked, I'm a female."

"Chill out," Yannick said. "They're just words."

I pointed at Yannick's headphones on the stool. "Listening to music can change your whole mood. It can make a bad day good again. Can't it?"

Yannick shrugged. "Yeah."

"You can't have it both ways," I said. "You can't want words to mean something sometimes and then say that they're *just words* other times. Words are powerful."

"Why do girls have to get so dramatic?" Isaac scoffed. "Don't take things so seriously."

I narrowed my eyes at Isaac.

"Enough talk. Let's play something. Anything," Harold said.

"Maybe we should practise 'Free Heart,'" Isaac said. "Since Ana can't seem to even remember the words to that one."

I didn't really have an answer to that.

"Good idea," Trey said. "But we're working on my songs at some point. We have to. Otherwise, we've got no fresh material. No fresh material, no more Friday night gigs."

As the band started to play "Free Heart," something gnawed at me. But I couldn't put my finger on it. I channelled all my frustration into my performance, belting out the chorus line, "I'll never let anything chain this free heart." And that's when it hit me.

The sneaking around behind their backs. The lies.

My heart felt anything but free.

Chapter 12

A Warning

Monday night was the opening of Central High's production of *Grease*. Harold and I sat on a small platform at the back of the dark gym. On the tables in front of us was our sound gear. From our seats, we could see the back of the audience and the stage. I had the script in front of me, just in case I forgot the cues to the sound effects.

During the first intermission, parents mingled with their coffees from the concession window. I could hear them raving about how great the actors were, but nothing about our sound design. They seemed to think the sounds appeared out of thin air. No one realized how much work was involved. Who knew that the two of us in the back corner had spent hours of our free time designing the effects and timing all the songs?

If my parents were here, they would know. My dad would probably say something like, "What actors? All I could focus on was how realistic the sound effects were! What superstar music producer made those?" And he would say it obnoxiously loud, too. Just to show me how proud he was. It used to embarrass me, but I would love to hear it right now.

"Is that Gill?" Harold asked.

Sitting in one of the rows was a head of black curly hair. It looked like Gill, but I couldn't see enough of his face. I stepped down off the platform and walked along the wall to get a better view.

"Gill?" I called out.

He flashed me one of his big smiles. "If it isn't the real star of the play, working her sound magic! All your hard work has paid off. The effects are so realistic! And you've thought out the acoustics perfectly. Congratulations!"

"Thanks," I beamed. Finally, someone who appreciated me. "What are you doing here? Is someone you know in the play?"

"Yeah," he said. "You."

A busy guy like Gill came just to see me? I felt honoured. But I thought it was only fair to warn him: "You know, I only sit back there in the dark corner."

"That's okay," he said. "I can still enjoy your work, can't I?"

"How did you know about this?" I asked.

He laughed. "You told me, remember? May fifteenth, you said. I made a note of it. I knew your parents couldn't be here. Or your brother. Can't have you all alone with no one to share your night."

After school the next day, Harold and I took turns quizzing each other for a Biology test. We sat at his kitchen table while his mom mixed us a pitcher of iced tea at the counter.

"Who was the man talking to you last night?" Harold's mom asked me.

"Gill Daring," Harold answered. "The owner of the Showcase. He's the one who gave us the gig."

"Gill Daring. Yes, I've heard of him." His mom set the pitcher on the table with two glasses. Harold got up to use the bathroom. His mom waited until he was out of the room before saying to me, "Harold says you've been able to set up some amazing things for the band. A contract. An interview. A spot at the big festival."

"Yeah, things are happening," I said. I thanked her for the iced tea and poured myself a glass.

"How did you manage to get so much going for the band? It's all happened quite suddenly," she asked.

I took a long, slow sip of my iced tea.

"I imagine Gill played a big part of it all," she said. "He's very powerful on the local music scene."

"He's been a big help," I admitted. But I didn't want to talk about Gill. How would I explain how much he'd done for me and the band? I had promised him that I would keep the coaching and the gifts a secret.

When Harold returned, his mom asked him, "Could you leave us alone for a few more minutes?"

Suddenly I got a weird feeling. What was going on?

She waited until Harold's footsteps faded to the basement. Then she looked at me, and I could feel my palms turn sweaty.

She leaned close to me and put her hands on my forearm. "Ana, I promised your mother

I'd keep an eye on you while she's away. I need to ask you something. Is anything going on between you and Gill Daring?"

I shook my head, embarrassed. "Of course not."

"These things he's doing for the band," she said. "Does he ever expect things in return?"

I didn't like the sound of her voice. It was as if she was warning me that a dangerous storm was coming and I better take cover.

Before I could answer, she went on. "Usually we think of abuse as something that happens suddenly. When an abusive man gets angry, for example, and hits his girlfriend. But some men will spend a long time preparing a woman to become their victim. It's called grooming. Men like that are excellent at fooling everyone. Masters at manipulation. That way, the victim doesn't even know what he's doing until it's too late."

Why was she telling me this?

"If you ever need to talk to anyone — about

anything — I'm always here for you. I hope you know that, Ana."

I nodded and mumbled, "Thanks."

"And one other thing," she added. "I know you're a very smart young lady. And I know you pride yourself on being independent. You've had to be, since your parents have been away so often the past few years. And with Jose working all the time. But anyone can become a victim of grooming, Ana. Anyone. It doesn't mean you're dumb. Or gullible."

Harold was heading back up the stairs.

His mom added under her breath, "Anyone who thinks they can't become a victim is making a dangerous mistake."

That night I opened my phone to look at the photos I took of Trey's new song lyrics. I wondered about my conversation with Harold's mom. Where did it come from? Maybe she'd seen the post from Melissa Smith on the Showcase's Facebook page. She could have been checking the comments about our band. Or someone could have told her about it because of her job at the Women's Crisis Centre. After years of working in a place like that, it made sense that she would be paranoid.

But she didn't know what Gill was really like. If she'd only seen how much the whole town loved him. Or how grateful the homeless people were that he spent his time delivering food to them. He had not spoken kindly to that one man, but there was probably a good reason. Maybe the man had done something to Gill. Who knew? But Gill had done nothing to make me uncomfortable. We were friends. And he was my music coach. I was smart enough to know if someone was manipulating me.

I read through Trey's lyrics again. I started to think Gill was right. I was going to quickly outgrow the rest of Shadow Beat. I remembered what the guys had said about me. Dramatic. Sensitive. They had called me those things as if I were weak. I couldn't decide. Should I stand up against the demeaning lyrics?

Or show them I was tough enough to not care about a few stupid words. But the bottom line was that I wanted to have some control over the direction the band was heading. Since I couldn't control the lyrics, I was going to control the music. Opening my DAW, I started playing around with synth sounds. If we were going to perform these songs, the least I could do was make the tracks kick ass.

Chapter 13

Red Flags

"Let's open tonight's show with 'Cavern,'" Trey suggested.

We were getting set up on stage.

"Are we ready to play it?" Harold asked.

"Hell, yeah, we are," Isaac said. He played a short riff on his bass guitar.

"What do you think, Ana?" Harold asked.

The Wednesday before, I had shown up at rehearsal with all the music for Trey's songs. As usual, the guys thought my tracks were incredible. We had practised hours that night. And the next day we all skipped the afternoon of school to practise more.

I said, "We might sound rough. But we could explain to the audience that we're testing out a few new numbers. They won't expect it to be polished. I've seen bands do it all the time."

"Then it's settled," Trey said. "'Cavern' first."

"Can we at least take out the word 'whore' for that one?" I asked.

Trey rolled his eyes. "I thought we agreed not to change anything."

"I just —" I sighed. "I feel stupid having to sing that part with you."

"What's the big deal?" Yannick asked. "You listen to the same kind of stuff."

"Yeah, you listen to Kanye West all the time," Trey said. "His songs are full of these kinds of lyrics."

Isaac nodded. "And you like Ashnikko. Her lyrics are pretty rude. In fact, they're demeaning to guys. She even has a song called 'Stupid Boy.'"

"That's different," I said.

But I knew they had a point. I did listen to music with lyrics similar to Trey's. How could I complain, then? How could I describe to them that it felt different when I performed lyrics that put down women? How could I describe to them what it felt like to sing those lyrics with guys who were supposed to be my friends?

The Showcase was packed again. Gill stood behind the coffee counter, waiting to hear the fresh material we had promised. When the lights flooded the stage, the crowd clapped and whistled loudly.

Our new song "Cavern" opened with Trey's voice only, no instruments.

"Baby, I wanna explore your cavern . . ."

I added background vocals. "Cavern, cavern, cavern."

I felt like a complete idiot singing a song about vaginas. Normally Trey was a great writer.

But this was a terrible metaphor. His next lines talked about caverns as if they were something to be conquered. Like climbing a mountain. About how he wanted to enter as many caverns as he could, counting the numbers in his black book.

I tried not to cringe as I sang. I hoped those three girls who had talked to me about becoming musicians weren't in the crowd tonight. What would they think of this new song? Would they think I was a sellout? Or would they love it?

No doubt the crowd loved it. Several people swarmed onto the dance floor with their arms high in the air. The second verse was twice as long as the first. It called for Trey to rap at lightning speed. When Trey nailed it perfectly, the crowd went wild. By the second chorus, the audience was singing along, "Cavern, cavern, cavern!"

"Get Down on This" got an even bigger reaction from the crowd. During the song, Trey got bolder with his gestures on stage. As he rapped about blow jobs, he grabbed his crotch several times. A table full of women hollered encouragement.

The energy in the Showcase was at an all-time high. Despite hating the lyrics we were singing, I had never felt so much adrenaline on stage. Still, this wasn't how I imagined my music. I wanted to express messages that lifted people up. Messages that made people feel powerful. These songs made me feel used and worthless.

I was relieved to finally get through all three new songs. We switched to some older songs, starting with "How Much Is Too Much?" Trey and I shared the singing on that song, playing it as a duet. Happy to sing something I believed in, I performed my vocals better than I ever had before. I hoped it would make Gill happy.

After the show, people asked Trey if the new songs were online yet.

"They will be soon!" Trey promised. He looked at me. I took care of the band's social media and SoundCloud uploads. Except for texting and posting Instagram photos, Trey wasn't much of a techie. "We'll get them recorded and posted this weekend, eh, Ana?"

I shrugged and nodded. *Whatever.*

A guy approached me. I recognized him from Math class but couldn't remember his name.

"Great show," he said.

"Thanks," I said.

"My favourite was 'How Much Is Too Much?'" he said.

I perked up a little.

He sat down on the edge of the stage. "I play baseball. I'm a pitcher for the Ravens."

Right. I remembered his name. Jordie Cole. I'd seen his picture in the sports section of the local paper.

"I practise throwing balls through a tire swing for, like, four hours a day," he said. "All my friends give me a hard time for not hanging out with them. But I got a dream, you know?"

"I definitely know," I said.

Along with "Free Heart" and "Fiercely Independent," "How Much Is Too Much?" was a really personal song for me. It was about being devoted to your dreams at all costs. Like Jordie, I'd sacrificed hundreds of hours of hanging out with friends to practise over the years.

"Anyway, just wanted to tell you I loved the song," Jordie said as he hopped off the stage. "It really spoke to me."

I watched him walk away. A huge smile crossed my face. This was one of the reasons I wrote music. To connect with others.

✳✳✳

On the way home from the show, I pulled the truck into my favourite spot overlooking the beach. It was dark and the half moon was faint behind the clouds. It was probably too late for caffeine. But I sipped on a frappuccino I'd bought at the coffee shop drive-thru.

As I watched a silver-haired man walk along the shore with his terrier, I checked my phone. No texts, but there was a notification that I had two Facebook messages. When I opened them, the messages were both from the same person. But it wasn't anyone I knew. There was no photo. Only a blank avatar. Lyla Jones. I knew that name from somewhere. But where?

The first message read: Sometimes it seems easier for women to just say "yes" even when they don't want to. But there is another way. #MeToo

The second message was sent an hour after the first. It read: You are being groomed. Don't believe me? Look for the red flags.

Then I remembered where I'd seen the name before. In the Facebook comments about Melissa Smith. Lyla Jones was the one who had written *MeToo*. How did Lyla Jones get hold of me? And what the hell was going on? First a false accusation on Facebook. Then Harold's mom overreacting to Gill's help. Now this. I felt terrible for women who were abused and assaulted, of course I did. But that was not happening to me. Not even close.

Chapter 14

Another Favour

I awoke and remembered — it was Harold's big day. The day he got his new Yamaha drum set. Two years before, he had taped a magazine photo of those drums to his locker door at school. I was happy for him so, of course, I promised to help him get the new kit home in my pickup truck. Afterward, I planned to stay and set it up with him. He'd be excited to have someone there to hear it for the first time. I took a shower and got ready to head downtown with him.

Once I was out of the shower, I read the text I missed. It was from Gill.

Did you forget we had a meeting?

Gill's message confused me. A meeting? For the life of me, I couldn't recall us having plans to meet. Before answering, I scrolled up through the older messages but there was nothing. No mention of plans.

I texted, I'm sorry. I did forget. What time was it?

11. My office. I've been waiting.

The thing about texting was that, unless the person used an emoji, it was hard to figure out how they were feeling. I worried that Gill was upset with me. It was quarter after eleven. If I hustled, I could get there in ten minutes.

Be right there. I'm out the door.

I left in such a rush that it wasn't until I was halfway up the highway when I remembered Harold. My heart sank. He was probably standing at his window with the curtains held open. Tapping his foot impatiently and dreaming about the drum kit waiting for him at the music store.

The second I parked, I texted Harold.

Going to be late. Sorry. Forgot I had something first. I'll text again when I'm on my way.

I hurried into Gill's office. I tried to catch my breath as I apologized.

Gill held up his hand for me to stop. "It's okay. Relax. I caught up on some paperwork. We need to discuss the photo shoot on Monday. Verna Huygens will be doing your makeup first, so you need to be here at one."

"One? But I have a Biology test right after lunch on Monday."

Gill sighed. "Do you want to become a biologist or a musician?"

"A musician," I said.

Not a big deal, I thought. I could phone in sick on Monday. That way, Ms. Semple would let me take the test on Tuesday. "I'll be there," I promised.

"That's my girl," Gill said. Then he grimaced and stretched his neck. "Tim Strider is the photographer. The café doesn't open until three tomorrow, so we'll do the photo shoot out in the main area. We can use the music gear if we want. Bring your guitar."

I agreed. But then I got anxious. A makeup artist? A real photographer? That stuff didn't come cheap. Maybe I could borrow the money from Jose.

"We need good lead time to market your performances at the festival. We've got just over two months. I hope you've been reworking your material to go solo. I mean, we'll get you a backup band. But you'll want a fresh set of songs."

"Backup band? Can't I just use Shadow Beat?"

"You need a more solid band to back you up. A more mature group."

This felt like a punch in my gut. It was one thing to imagine a solo act in addition to our Shadow Beat set. But the guys would be furious to see that my solo act was a full band. Minus them.

"Could I at least use Harold as my drummer?"

Gill grimaced again and rubbed his neck. "I hate to say it, Ana. But if you want to make it in this business, you need to drop some baggage. You can't get caught up in your feelings. Hanging out with Harold is going to make it that much harder when you have to cut your ties with him. My advice? Start drifting away from him now. It'll make it easier in the long run."

My life was changing before my eyes, and I wasn't sure how I felt about it. Everything was slipping from my hands. At the same time, I was grabbing for something bigger. Was it worth it if I had to lose my friends? I couldn't imagine not being best friends with Harold. Maybe Gill was right. There was no place for feelings in this business.

Now Gill rubbed his neck with both hands. "The new songs you played last night. Were those yours? Or Trey's?"

Was he serious? Did he actually think I'd write lyrics like those?

"By the shocked look on your face," he said with a smile, "I'm guessing they were Trey's. Figures. Immature crap. I hate those kind of lyrics. So demeaning to women. But your songs, Ana, are sophisticated, uplifting. Your songs connect with listeners. I can see it in the audience's reaction. Trey's songs only connect with his penis."

I stifled a laugh. Hearing someone else say that about Trey's lyrics made me feel lighter inside. Like I had an ally. Sure, Harold had sided with me. But he wasn't in the music business. Not like Gill was anyway.

Gill moved his neck from side to side, his face twisting in pain.

"Are you okay?" I asked.

"I think I did something when I was

looking for that Percy Sledge record for you," he said. "I had to move some heavy crates to get at it. And then I made it worse unloading those sandwiches the other day. Haven't been able to sleep."

"Sorry to hear that," I said. "Hope you feel better soon."

"If I could loosen it somehow. Hey, do you think you —" He stopped.

"What?" I asked.

"Never mind," he said. "It's too much to ask."

"No, no. Go ahead," I said.

He snapped his fingers. "Hold on a second. Before I forget, the makeup and photo shoot will cost eight hundred dollars. But I don't want you to worry. I've got it covered for you. Poster costs, too."

I was floored. "I don't know what to say. Thank you."

Gill grimaced again. "I know it's a big request . . . Do you think you could work this kink out of my neck for me?"

I stared at him. The idea of rubbing his neck weirded me out.

"Please? I wouldn't ask if it wasn't killing me," he said.

I didn't know what to do. The longer I stood there, the more awkward I felt. I tried to tell myself that it wasn't that big a deal. I would be helping somebody in pain. Simple as that.

Standing behind his chair, I looked at the back of his neck and took a deep breath. No matter what I tried to tell myself, it felt too personal to touch the skin on the back of Gill Daring's neck.

"Something wrong?" he asked. His head was hanging forward.

"No," I said.

In my head I counted down from three and forced my hand to touch his neck. It jolted me a little, how his cool skin felt against mine. It didn't feel right. But I started to knead his muscles with my fingers. He let out a long moan. It startled me. Then another one.

Soon he was moaning constantly. It didn't seem like a moan of relief. It sounded almost sexual. But I might have been wrong. The poor guy was in pain. I needed to stop overthinking this.

Chapter 15

The Photo Shoot

For more than an hour I sat in a chair at the Showcase while Verna Huygens plastered my face with makeup and did my hair. When she held up a mirror for me to see, I didn't recognize myself. I mean, it was me but more . . . spectacular. Like someone who belonged on the cover of a magazine. Like the Shadow Santos I'd always imagined. Sexy. Fierce. Mysterious.

"You've got a good energy," Verna said. She was an older lady dressed in a funky purple outfit with piercings in her eyebrows and nose. "A strong vibe."

"Thanks." I turned this way and that to see myself from different angles in the mirror. Looking like this, I was ready to take on the world. "The hair, the makeup . . . it's perfect. You really get what I'm all about."

Verna leaned close to my face. She narrowed her eyes at me in a way that seemed playful. She smirked. "And what exactly are you all about, Ana? No, wait. Let me guess . . ." She stood upright again, then closed her eyes. She pressed her fingers against her temples, pretending to channel invisible energy. "An independent spirit. Confident. Cool. Calm."

I smiled. Did I really give off that energy? I hoped so. Handing Verna the mirror, I stood up and tugged the hairdressing cape off my neck. Nothing like a makeover and a handful of compliments to lift you up. I swore I was two inches taller.

"Just be careful not to flatten your hair when you change into your outfit," Verna said.

"Oh, I'm already dressed," I replied. I was wearing my fake leather pants with the tall boots and my black tank top.

The front door opened and the photographer came in with his cameras and lenses. The lighting had been set up earlier. Around the stage there were white umbrellas tilted on stands to reflect the light evenly.

"Gill had a wardrobe rack brought in for you," Verna said. "You'll pick something from that. He's very choosy about what his musicians wear. Trust him. He knows what he's doing."

As I headed down the hall toward Gill's office, I checked my phone. When I left the Showcase on Saturday, Harold had texted me before I had a chance to say that I was finally on my way.

Don't bother coming. I went with Trey to get my drums.

He hadn't been in touch with me since. Not even to answer the fifteen texts I'd sent. Was this his way of telling me that he'd had enough of me not showing up? The whole thing sat like a stone in my stomach. I should have been there for him.

A clothes rack on wheels sat in the middle of Gill's office. Most of the clothes were black. There were flashes of purple and red mixed in there.

Gill leaned sideways in his chair to see past the wardrobe rack. "I told them at the rental shop to give me clothes for a superstar who calls herself Shadow. Turns out one of them had seen you perform here. Said he was a big fan. He was excited to pick these out for you."

"Wow, this is so cool!" I pulled the hangers apart to look at each outfit. I wanted to wear them all. I chose a tight black leather vest with a black silk blouse underneath. The blouse had a huge ruffled collar that reminded me of Prince. I also grabbed a black skirt that looked like a kilt full of safety pins. Plus some chunky military boots with a dozen buckles. A punk-rock-meets-Prince kind of vibe. I loved to mix styles of clothing as much as I loved to mix styles in music.

Gill explained, "A buddy of mine runs a rental store. He loans out clothes and props to movie sets. I can get hold of anything. You could wear a new outfit each night."

I changed in the washroom. I loved how the blouse ruffles clung tight and high around my neck when I buttoned it to the top. And how the leather vest cinched around my waist. Classy and sexy.

When I returned, Gill looked me over. Without a word, he undid the buttons of the blouse until I was nothing but cleavage.

"That's better," he said, fluffing the ruffles. "More like Shadow Santos."

Gill understood what made a musician popular. So I knew I should trust him, like Verna told me. But I couldn't stand being controlled like that.

"I like it better like this," I said, and did up the buttons. I had no problem with showing some skin. I had done it many times on stage. But I liked the ruffles framing my face. I looked like a combination of a Calvin Klein model and something out of *Alice in Wonderland*. It was quirky. It was me.

"You need to use your looks on the stage, Ana."

"I like how I look," I said.

"You look great," he agreed. "But music is sex. Sex sells. Simple as that. You have to use your sexuality to your advantage, Ana. And I know you're more than capable of doing that. You've given off that sex vibe every show. Every outfit you've worn on stage has shown the audience that you are ready for sex. Which is a big reason why you caught my eye. It's what the crowd wants to feel from you. Why not make sure people see it in your posters, too?"

I had always been confident about how I dressed on stage. In that instant, it all vanished into thin air. Was that what people thought when they saw Shadow Santos on stage? I'm ready for sex? That wasn't why I dressed that way.

Gill moved in and undid the buttons again. "Think about sex."

"What?" I took a step backwards.

"Think about sex during the photo shoot," Gill said. "Trust me. It's a little trick many of my musicians have used. It'll give your eyes a dreamy look. It will drive a big crowd to your show at the festival."

I felt the blood rush into my face. I couldn't decide whether to run out of there or take his advice. A big crowd at my show in the summer would be amazing.

"Are you experienced enough to think about sex?" Gill asked.

"Uh . . . yeah," I stammered, completely shocked by the question.

"With boys, I bet," he said. "Not with a *man*."

I didn't like how he stressed the last word, as if he was hinting at something. The awkward memory of rubbing his sore neck on Saturday popped into my head. I worried he was about to ask me for more than a massage. But it turned out I had nothing to worry about. I should've thought better of Gill. He wasn't like that.

He said, "Remember, this is a tough business. But it will be easier if you listen to me. I'm here to coach you. Now, you better get out there. Timothy's probably waiting for you. Remember: sex."

✱✱✱

The photo shoot went smoothly, but it was tiring to hold so many different poses for an hour. Timothy seemed pleased with my energy and my facial expressions. Though not once did I take Gill's advice. There was no way I could make myself think about sex while staring at a man I had just met five minutes earlier. Instead, I saw myself as a famous musician who wasn't afraid to be what she wanted to be. A musician who could wear what she wanted to wear without the crowd thinking she was ready for sex.

After, I went back to Gill's office. He watched me from his desk as I grabbed my clothes off the couch. I started to head back to the hall.

"Where are you going?" Gill asked.

"Washroom," I said. "To get changed."

Gill shook his head. "Stay here."

"All right," I said. I thought he must have business to discuss.

He looked me over from head to toe. "I mean, you can change here."

"Thanks, but that's okay," I said. "Just as easy to change in the washroom. I don't want to kick you out of your office."

"I wasn't planning to leave," he said with a smirk.

I clutched my ball of clothes tight against my chest.

"Go on," Gill said. "Get those clothes off."

I took a few steps toward the door.

"Not in the washroom," he said. His voice was sharp and sounded mean. It was the tone he used when he talked to that homeless guy. The voice of a guy who got what he wanted, no matter what someone else thought. "Change here."

I stumbled on my words. "I — I don't want to."

Gill stood up. "Are you thankful for everything I've done for you, Ana?"

"Of course," I said quietly.

"Then show me how thankful you are," he said. "I'm not asking for much. Just a peek."

Gill's smirk was creeping me out. I inched my way toward the door.

"You owe me," he said calmly. "I scratch your back and you scratch mine."

"I need to go," I said.

Gill motioned at the couch. "Get naked and let me get a good look."

I clenched my jaw and shook my head. For a moment, I felt unable to move. Then Gill unzipped his pants. I didn't wait to see if he meant to touch me or not. Every muscle in my body flexed. As I flung the door wide open, he called out after me.

"Your career is over if you walk out now."

I didn't walk.

I ran.

Chapter 16

A Daring Request

By the time I got home, I was exhausted. My eyes were swollen from crying. I shuddered at the thought of what Gill planned to do to me. It didn't matter if all he wanted was to see my naked body this time. And jerk off to the sight of it. It was clear that he thought he deserved sex with me, now or later.

Harold's mom was right about Gill. I felt stupid for not seeing it. After changing out of the borrowed clothes, I checked to see if Harold had texted me. I wanted to tell him what had happened, but I was embarrassed. Harold's mom had been right. Maybe Harold thought I knew what I was getting into. And the other guys in the band. All along, I had no idea what Gill wanted from me. So was it my fault for not thinking that I would have to pay some day, some way?

No text from Harold. But I had received a message from another stranger. This time it was a woman named Ramead Ngozi. Her photo showed a young woman just a few years older than me.

I've seen your shows. You're an amazing musician. I want to discuss an opportunity with you. Meet me for coffee?

Do I know you? I responded.

I could see that she was online. She replied right away.

No. Let's meet somewhere public. The Java Shack? Tomorrow at four?

I was dying to know what kind of opportunity she had for me. My first thought was what Gill would say. It was automatic. But after what happened, why should I care what Gill thought?

I looked back at Ramead's message. Should I be excited? Or suspicious? After all, it might not be a woman at all. It might be some creepy guy who watched one of my shows. Suddenly, I wondered if anyone saw me as a talented musician. Maybe all anyone would want from me was sex.

I hated that Gill had made me so paranoid. The least I could do was show up. Spy through the Java Shack windows before going inside. If Ramead turned out to be a middle-aged man with a greasy moustache, then I'd take off.

I responded, See you then.

✳✳✳

When I reached the Java Shack the next day, I stood outside and peeked through the windows. There were about a dozen people seated around the tables. I recognized Ramead Ngozi from the photo in the message. She was seated in the corner. As I watched her jot something in her notebook, I recognized Ramead as the young woman who nodded at me in the Showcase the day I met with Gill for the first time.

I felt hopeful. This might be a legit opportunity.

I walked into the coffee shop and headed to Ramead's table. As I approached, Ramead looked up and gave me a small nod. Just like on that day in the Showcase, her expression looked serious.

Ramead shook my hand. "Glad you could make it."

I sat down. I was excited to hear about the music opportunity.

"I'm going to get straight to the point," Ramead said. "I want you to join our local *#MeToo* movement to stop Gill Daring. To stop him from sexually harassing women."

Stunned, I flopped back in my chair. "This isn't about my music?"

"It *is* about your music," she said. "It's about your right to be a part of the music business without giving up your body. Or your dignity. It's about your music, and it's about mine. It's about us clearing a new path for other musicians."

"You're a musician?" I asked.

"I was. Friday night gigs at ten o'clock."

"What do you play?" I asked.

"My mouth. I'm a beatboxer. Two-time North American champ."

"Wow." I was impressed. "So how come you're not there anymore?"

Lifting her notebook, Ramead said, "We need to stop him. I've been mounting a case against him. Talking with other victims. The more of us who speak out, the better."

"I think you've got the wrong person," I said. A day later, I was still confused about what had happened with Gill. I had fooled myself into believing Gill didn't want anything in return for helping me with my career. But it didn't make me a victim. Just stupid.

"Justice triumphs when brave voices come together," Ramead said. "We're going to report Gill Daring to the police and the newspapers."

I thought about Gill's office. He had told me to undress. He had unzipped his pants. But nothing had happened in the end. Besides, maybe I had given Gill the wrong idea about us. "Report him? For what?"

"Has Gill given you any gifts?" Ramead flipped to a blank page.

I stared at the notebook as she wrote *Jane Doe 5* at the top of the page.

"Gifts that he asked you to keep secret?" she asked.

"Whatever this is," I said, "it's got nothing to do with me."

"Has he offered to coach you?" she asked. "Told you that you're friends?"

"So what?" I asked. My voice still sounded sharp.

"How about favours? Does he do favours for you? And then ask you for small favours in return?"

"Yes," I said. "But —"

She made a note in her book, nodding to herself. "He's not just sexually harassing women anymore. There are too many accusations, and he has to be careful. We think he's changed his strategy. Have you ever heard of grooming?"

I had. From Harold's mom. But I didn't feel like answering. I had a funny feeling that I was going to regret this meeting.

Ramead lowered her voice. "Grooming is when someone works to create a relationship with a person — usually a child or a young person like yourself. Usually it's a friendship or a coaching relationship. The person builds trust so they can manipulate and abuse their victim. Sexually."

"Wait. Why are you telling me this?"

"He's grooming you, Ana."

I laughed, then shook my head. "I'm not a victim. I haven't had sex with Gill. Nothing happened."

"It's hard to see when you're being groomed. Until it's too late."

"You're wrong," I said. "Gill's not like that." I still believed that, didn't I?

"People like Gill," she said, "are chameleons. They can change their colours very easily. You're not the first person to think that someone couldn't be a sexual predator because he's a 'nice' guy."

"Look," I said. "I'd know if someone was grooming me."

"Grooming is a very slow process," Ramead said. "Some people are groomed for years. You're lucky to be catching it this early."

I was getting embarrassed. But I tried to remain calm. "Let's say Gill has been grooming me. Why me?"

"There are certain signs they'll look for

when targeting a victim."

I felt empty inside. It wasn't true. Gill was my coach. We were friends. Somewhere along the way I had given Gill the wrong idea about us. It was just a misunderstanding. I mean, there *was* the neck rub. But that wasn't really sexual. Had I made it seem like I wanted to be more than friends? I looked at Ramead. "So you're saying there's something about me that makes me a good victim?"

Ramead got flustered. "No, that's not what I mean at all. It's not your fault, Ana. And what happened to me wasn't my fault either. Though it's taken me a lot of therapy sessions to accept that."

I didn't want to ask what happened to her. To be honest, I was nervous about hearing her answer. For the same reason I was scared to catch sight of one of the women at the place where Harold's mom worked. So I went at the question sideways. "How come you don't play at the Showcase anymore?"

"Because Gill Daring sexually assaulted me in his office."

I didn't want to believe her. But this wasn't someone hiding behind a fake name and a blank avatar. This was a real person. And I got the sense that she wasn't the type to make up something like this. Then again, if what she said about Gill was true, I wasn't exactly good at reading people. I felt like such an idiot. I pictured the leather couch in Gill's office. I thought of my research on the *#MeToo* movement — those casting couches where actors had sex with powerful people so they could make it in show business.

"So it was you who put the sticker on my guitar case?" I asked.

"Sorry about that. I needed to reach out to you. But it never works when I try to approach girls too soon. They just deny that anything is happening."

"Girls? More than one?"

Ramead nodded. "Gill Daring has taken

advantage of his influence to harass and assault female musicians at the Showcase. We figure he got scared of getting caught. That's why he shifted his strategy to grooming his victims. It's much harder to prove grooming than assault."

If it's so hard to prove, I thought, *then Ramead could be wrong about me.* Nothing Gill had done seemed like sexual harassment or abuse.

"We can't let him get away with this anymore," Ramead said. "Once some of us talk, more women will find the courage. Everyone knows this goes on. They just don't talk about it. That's why they call these situations open secrets. Secrets everyone knows about, but pretend they don't. It's why I hang out in the Showcase. To show him that I'm watching him."

I couldn't imagine going back to a place where I'd been assaulted. But I hadn't got up the nerve to return the borrowed clothes either.

"Ana, would you at least be willing to meet

the reporter covering this?" Ramead asked. "Your report would be anonymous, since you're a minor. You could just be Jane Doe Five."

I shook my head. "I have nothing to report."

"Give it some thought," Ramead said. "It's taken me some time before I've become ready to report it to the police."

"If you're going to the police, what do you need me for?" I asked.

"I'm worried there's not enough evidence," Ramead admitted. "Especially when it comes to a powerful guy like Gill. A lot of other powerful people will come to his defence. The more voices that speak out and report this, the better. Make it so that the police can't ignore it." Ramead rested her hand gently on top of her notebook. She leaned toward me and looked straight into my eyes. "I promise you, Ana. If you decide to do this, you'll be helping a lot of other girls."

***

In my bedroom, I fell onto my bed and buried my face in my pillow. I felt like crying. But no tears came. I was too shocked and it made me numb all over. I still refused to believe that I was being groomed. Wouldn't I have seen the signs? The red flags, as Lyla Jones had messaged to me. Lyla Jones. Ramead Ngozi. How many others had been watching me?

Anyway, so what if Gill and I exchanged a few innocent favours? That's the way the world worked. You couldn't expect to get things from people and not ever try to return the favour. But what if Harold was right? What if I did act like I was invincible? How had his mom put it? "Anyone who thinks they can't become a victim is making a dangerous mistake." If that were true, this was all my fault. I was to blame — for trying to be *too* confident.

Everything I'd kept bottled up during my meeting with Ramead suddenly burst out of me.

I couldn't control it. My chest heaved with sobs. I really needed my parents right now. All my pretending that I was in control — it was just a cover for missing my parents so damn much. I climbed off the bed and opened Skype on my computer. I tried to video call them, not caring that they would see me crying. No answer. Everyone seemed to believe that teenagers wanted nothing to do with their parents. But the truth was, this was when I needed them most.

Chapter 17

A Tough Decision

I researched grooming on my computer that night. To be honest, I felt guilty looking it up. As if I was saying that Gill was guilty when nothing had really happened to me. But what might have happened to me if I hadn't ran out?

Here I thought this whole time I was becoming sophisticated Shadow Santos. But really, I was only ever stupid, gullible Ana. The least I could do now was try to understand what grooming was. *Knowledge is power*, I thought, *or something like that*.

At first I only read through the articles I found online. After a while, my head was swimming with information. So I grabbed some paper and started to make notes. From what I could make out, the first step of grooming a victim was to establish a friendship. Building a friendship caused the victim to let down their guard.

The perpetrator — usually called the "perp" for short — would build the friendship by finding out what the victim liked. Gill and I both liked soul music, but that didn't mean anything. Lots of people liked the same kind of music.

According to one website, the perp often uses social media to find out what their victim likes. I opened my Instagram account and looked at the post about the Percy Sledge album Harold found. Part of my caption read: *Only need to hunt down the* Warm and Tender

Soul *album to complete my collection. Impossible to find.*

I never told Gill Daring about needing the *Warm and Tender Soul* album. He must have been on my social media. At the time, I thought it was a funny coincidence that we both collected soul music records.

I read that perps look for other ways to connect with the victim, like dropping the names of people they both know. Gill and I didn't know any of the same people outside of Shadow Beat. Wait a second. There was our conversation about school. That's when Gill said that he remembered Jose. But they did go to school together. Wasn't that a normal thing to mention?

I guessed that, put together, these could be the red flags Lyla Jones was talking about. But did it really mean Gill was grooming me to be a victim?

Then I forced my mind back to what happened in his office. I was pretty sure unzipping his pants and telling me to change in front of him was a red flag. I scrapped my page of notes and grabbed a fresh sheet of paper. On it, I started a diagram to map out my time with Gill.

Once the friendship was started, the perp uses favours and promises to build trust. On my diagram, I listed Gill's promises. The Friday night gig. A spot at the Endless Summer Festival. Plus, he had offered to pay for my photo shoot and marketing costs.

Favours and promises make the victim feel like they owe the perp. The first favours are usually something fairly small. Like a soul album.

As the list grew, it all started to fall into place. What an idiot I was for feeling so special.

The perp finds silly reasons for keeping even the small gifts a secret from everybody else. Secrets make the victim feel even more special. Flattered, too. I felt flattered for sharing a secret with somebody like Gill.

But the favours aren't one-way. Small favours are asked of the victim, too. Like borrowing my truck to deliver sandwiches.

Once a pattern of exchanging favours is set, it slowly leads to sexual favours. Or favours that seemed almost sexual. Like a neck massage. Then things that *were* sexual. Like asking to see me undress. Like unzipping his pants.

Perps also find ways to become part of the victim's daily life. Gill did text me often, but that was always about business. Well, mostly. On one website there was an example that sent a shiver down the back of my neck. A perp came to events that other family members were unable to attend. Even at the time, I thought there was something strange about Gill showing up at my school's production of *Grease*. We had just met when he made note of the date.

I was starting to see red flags where I hadn't seen them before.

Then I got to the part about coaching, and my skin prickled. Coaching is a way of seeming generous to the victim. Plus, if the victim is getting coached in something they really want to get good at, they are excited for the attention. But what did that mean for me? Gill had said that he coached only the musicians with special talent. Was that just a lie? What if I wasn't as talented as Gill had said? After everything, I didn't know what was true and what was false — about anything.

The perp finds ways to separate the victim from friends and family. How many rehearsals had I missed because Gill texted me at the wrong time? I went to our band's Instagram page. I always posted what the band was up to. What we were rehearsing that evening and when. And hadn't Gill told me that I'd have to leave people behind? Including my best friend? I didn't want to think of all the lies Gill got me to tell Harold and the rest of the band.

By the time I finished my research, I had

a diagram of Gill's grooming. Now what was I going to do with it?

What would happen if I agreed to help Ramead? What would it mean for the band? For starters, our gig at the Showcase would get axed, plus our spot at the festival. What would the band say? They'd be furious. I used to think that the guys respected me, but now I wasn't so sure. Especially after hearing Trey's lyrics. Trey and the others could take their crappy lyrics and go do their own thing, for all I cared.

But Gill. That's who scared me. Would Gill come after me if he found out I helped Ramead? I wouldn't be named in the newspaper, Ramead had promised that. But Gill might have ways of figuring it out.

I searched *#MeToo* again. This time I scrolled through the hundreds of tweets from women who had joined the movement online. Some women said how ashamed they felt after being assaulted by a man they trusted. Others said that they had believed they deserved it.

But now they realized it wasn't their fault. I kept wondering if I was to blame. Had I done something to lead Gill on? Many women said that no one believed them. Many people sided with their abuser by saying things like, "But I know him. He'd never do anything like that." How many times had I told myself that? Didn't I tell Ramead just that about Gill?

I hadn't been assaulted. But I couldn't shake the feeling that I had been in danger. Enough danger to have to leave. Now I was glad I trusted that feeling. And it was comforting to know that many women had had similar thoughts and feelings.

I remembered signing that contract. How Harold had complained that I always try to do everything on my own. This time, I wasn't going to act alone. I didn't have to do everything on my own. If these women could speak out, I could, too. Even if it ruined my music career.

I texted Ramead.

I'll speak to the reporter.

Fifteen minutes later, my phoned buzzed. It was Ramead.

Meet us at the Java Shack tomorrow at 4.

Chapter 18

Speaking Out

I was the first to arrive at the Java Shack. I got myself a vanilla latte and took a seat at the table where I had met Ramead. I was nervous and kept scanning the coffee shop. As if Gill Daring might be there. But there were only customers reading books and complaining about work.

Ramead walked in. She was followed by Samantha Thanh, the reporter who interviewed Shadow Beat at the Showcase. I put the pieces together as I recalled the questions Samantha had asked us. Her questions about the rumours in the music business. About whether Gill had asked us to trade more than our talent and creativity. Those questions were meant for me.

"Good to see you again, Ana," Samantha said. She took out her notebook and clicked her pen open. "What can I call you in the article? Jane Doe Five?"

I looked at Ramead.

"It's okay," Samantha said. "I know it's scary, but you won't be alone. There'll be many voices — some named, some not. Either way, no one will recognize your part in this report. But everyone's part is important."

Ramead nodded. "You're doing a brave thing, Ana. We all are."

Ramead took a small package of tissues from her bag and placed them down in the middle of the table. Obviously she was expecting me to cry at some point.

"This isn't just about you helping us with

the newspaper article," Samantha said. "We want to listen to you. To your story."

I nodded.

"Think back to when you first met Gill," Samantha said. "No detail is too small, Ana. This article is not only about exposing Gill. We want to educate people about the grooming process. What questions did he ask you during that first conversation?"

I thought for a moment. "He asked me if my parents wanted me home studying."

Samantha wrote it down. "And what did you say?"

"That my parents were in Mexico on business. Then he asked if it was hard to be on my own with them gone."

Ramead nodded. "He was trying to figure out who in your life might be aware of your relationship with him as it develops."

"Anything else from that first conversation?" Samantha asked.

"We talked about my dream of being a

musician," I said. "He wanted to know if I was serious, if it was my biggest dream."

"He knows that girls like you are driven by their dreams," Ramead said. "It makes it easier to lure with promises of a career. But it's not your fault, Ana. You didn't do a thing to deserve this."

"Did he give you gifts?" Samantha asked.

I nodded.

"Let me guess," Samantha said. "He gave you phony excuses why the gifts needed to be kept a secret?"

I didn't like to admit I'd bought such a stupid lie. "He told me not to let anybody know about the used record he gave me. He said other collectors would bug him for rare albums."

Ramead put her hand on my arm. "Don't be embarrassed, Ana. Perps like Gill are very careful and patient and clever. Someone with Gill's power and reputation can make you feel flattered for being trusted with a secret. People like him are very good at making a person feel special."

Samantha added, "And since he started with nonsexual favours and gifts, you don't think anything of it."

"Like I told you," Ramead said, "grooming is a very slow process. Some perps spend years grooming a victim."

I realized that Samantha was right. Why would anyone think a person is a sexual predator just because he gives you a used record? People would have thought I was overreacting. Even now, it was hard for me to clearly see where Gill's behaviour crossed the line. Especially when people talked about what a great guy Gill was.

"It's one of the reasons grooming is hard to prove," Samantha added. "Gill probably stopped sexually assaulting women because it's too easy to spot. Too easy to prove. He was taking his time with you, and probably thinks he'll never get caught."

When we finished, Ramead said, "Thank you

for your bravery. It's not easy to tell your story."

Between what I had researched and what Ramead and Samantha told me, I was starting to believe that it was true. That this could happen to anybody. They kept telling me that grooming is hard to see, even for the person being groomed. But part of me felt bad about my friendship with Gill all being a lie. Part of me still felt like it might have been my fault. Because a tiny part of me wondered how far I would have gone if I hadn't left Gill's office.

"This wasn't about you personally, Ana. Even though it feels very personal," Samantha said. "Men like Gill Daring thrive on using their power. Everything they do is about power."

Ramead nodded. "That's why he raped me. Not just for sex. But to show his power over me."

"You don't have to be raped to be scarred by this," said Samantha. "You were manipulated, Ana. If you hadn't figured it out when you did, it would have turned sexual."

"It did," I admitted. "Well, sort of. He wanted to watch me change. Then he —" I paused for a moment. "He unzipped his pants. But nothing happened. I ran out."

Samantha made a note. "But you can't stop thinking about what might have happened."

"We care about you, Ana. And we are here to help you any way we can." Samantha pulled out a business card and handed it to me. "This is a victim services organization. They offer counselling to women who have gone through this. It's easy to think that you don't need therapy. But you might. It can really help."

"Definitely consider it. It's helped me," Ramead said. "Pay attention to certain signs. Like if you start losing sleep. Or lose interest in the things you love. Or skip your responsibilities, like school."

I put the card in my pocket. "What happens now?"

Ramead explained, "Two of us went to the

police yesterday. We pressed charges against Gill Daring. We're hoping it will be enough to put him in jail."

Samantha closed her notebook and slid it into her bag. "You're my last interview for this news piece. It will be online this Thursday."

Chapter 19

Charges

I stayed home from school for the rest of the week. Trey and Isaac showed zero sympathy that I wasn't feeling well. That was okay by me, since I wasn't actually sick. I just needed time to recover from everything.

We're losing valuable practice time, Trey texted me several times.

I didn't feel like seeing them. And I didn't feel like playing music.

On Thursday, I got a call from the Showcase.

When I saw the call display, I froze and let it ring. After, I checked my voice mail. Whoever phoned me left a message. As soon as I heard the voice was female, I relaxed.

"Hi, Ana. It's Kalli. I'm phoning all the bands to let you know that we're going to be closed this Friday. So, no Friday night gig. Sorry about that. I'll keep you posted."

I wanted to ask Kalli if something happened to Gill. But I didn't want her to suspect I was a part of it. Samantha's article would be in the paper today. Maybe it would report whether Gill had been charged or not. Every fifteen minutes I checked online to see if it had been posted.

Just before dinner there was a knock on our front door. It was Harold. We hadn't talked since I ditched our trip to the music store. The fact that he wasn't smiling made me think he was still mad at me. Still, I was really happy to see him.

Clutched against his chest was his tablet. He turned it around and showed me a photo of the

Showcase with the headline: *The Showcase Closes Its Doors After Owner Faces Sexual Assault Charges.*

I felt so weak I had to brace myself against the wall.

"Do you want to read it?" Harold held out his tablet.

I shook my head. "Have you read it?"

"Not yet. I thought we could read it together."

"Read it first," I said. "Not out loud."

Harold sat at the kitchen table. I stood in the doorway and watched him read. I chewed on my thumbnail.

When Harold finished reading, he leaned back in the chair and lifted his eyebrows high. "Wow. That is one killer article. Gill is done."

"Was I mentioned?"

"No," he said. "You aren't in here." He didn't seem surprised by my question.

I let out a long breath. I sat down at the table and pulled the tablet closer to read the article. It said that more than fifteen women had made accusations against Gill for sexual harassment and sexual assault. Some of the women had identified themselves by their real names. Others, like Melissa Smith, used a fake name. And some were just Jane Does, like me. Most of the article focused on Ramead and a woman named Vivian Geller, who had pressed charges with the police.

No mention was made about the fate of the Showcase. It just said that its future was uncertain. And that its doors might remain closed for good.

"Guess we lost our gig," Harold said.

"I don't care," I said. "We'll find something better."

For a second my words surprised me. But I realized I was seeing things more clearly. I had lost a great chance at the Showcase. But I also knew that I had escaped that place before something terrible happened to me. It was a scary relief. Like almost stepping off the curb and seeing the speeding car just in time.

I tried to be positive. "I hope the band can bounce back from this."

"I don't," Harold said.

"You don't?"

"I think you and I should leave the band," Harold said.

I paced the kitchen floor. In my heart, I knew Harold was right. Harold and I had different ideas than the rest of the band. We had different ideas about what it meant to us. We wanted to write different kinds of songs from the ones Trey was writing.

"What do you think?" Harold asked.

"It's just hard to think of starting all over again," I said.

"I understand," Harold said. "You've been through a lot."

I whipped around. "You know?"

Harold nodded. "My mom talked to me. About what Gill was doing. How he was manipulating you. Pulling you away from your friends."

I looked down. "I'm so embarrassed."

"It could have happened to any of us. We were all excited by Gill's promises. It's not easy to stand up to someone who could make or break our dreams. Besides," Harold winked at me, "you're not invincible, you know."

Later that night the band met at Harold's. I walked into the basement to see the others slumped in their chairs in silence. On Trey's lap was his phone showing the newspaper article.

"This is a disaster," Trey moaned. "What are we going to do?"

"What can we do?" Yannick asked.

"I tell you what I'm doing," Trey said. "I'm speaking out."

"And saying what?" Harold asked.

Trey scowled. "That Gill is innocent. That this is a bunch of lies."

"How do you know he's innocent?" Harold asked.

"So you're on their side?" Isaac asked. "After everything Gill has done for us?"

Trey held up his phone. "My dad says there's no way this is true. Just some women trying to get money out of Gill."

"I don't think that's it," Harold said.

"My mom plays tennis with Gill's mom," Yannick said. "She says he's a really nice guy."

"What does that have to do with it?" Harold said.

"She knows him. He could never do something like this," Yannick said.

Harold rolled his eyes. "Guess she doesn't know him that well, then. Because he obviously *can* do something like this."

"Oh, come on," Isaac said. "How hard is it to make up lies?"

Harold laughed. "You think fifteen women got together to plan the same lie?"

"Actually, that's a good point," Yannick said. To my surprise, it sounded like he meant it. "If that many women have come forward, there's got to be something to it. I always thought Gill seemed a bit creepy."

Trey shook his head. "Bullshit."

"Ana and I are leaving Shadow Beat," Harold announced.

"What Harold means," I added, "is that you three are leaving Shadow Beat."

Trey stood up, his face bright red. "You can't do that."

"We can," I said. "We started this band. We auditioned you three guys for *our* band. Our time together is done."

Trey shook his head angrily. "No way —"

"Yes way," I said. "This is not Trey Beat. This is Shadow Beat. And I am Shadow Santos."

***

On the way home from Harold's house, I stopped at the Showcase. I needed to see for myself that it was truly shut down. I parked across the road about a half block down. I hunched behind the steering wheel and peered at the building. I tried to make out the words on the paper signs taped to the Showcase's front doors.

Temporarily closed. Our apologies.

It was true. It was closed.

I wasn't sure what I felt. I thought about the amazing times I'd had in that place. The crowd. The energy. The thrill of playing my music on stage. Yet it would always be a dark place in my mind, too. A place where a powerful man took advantage of people's dreams.

I was a different person now. That place had changed me. A lot of it for the better. I knew now why I always had to seem to be in control. It was because I hated having no control over my parents being away so much. And I knew now why I had been so scared of seeing those women at the centre where Harold's mom worked. Because in my heart I knew that it could happen to anyone. It had nothing to do with being strong or smart or independent.

Somebody from inside opened the door to the Showcase.

I ducked down behind the dashboard. Carefully, I lifted my head just enough to see out with one eye. It was Kalli. She locked the door to the darkened place and headed across the road. As Kalli walked up the sidewalk, she spotted me and waved.

I rolled down the window.

"What are you doing here?" Kalli asked.

"Uh." I got stuck. "Just shopping for some used books."

Kalli nodded, then motioned toward the café. "Can you believe all this?"

"Crazy," I said. "Think it will open again soon?"

"Soon?" She shook her head. "I doubt it ever will. I can't see Gill getting away with this."

I dangled my hand over the steering wheel. "Do you think he's guilty?"

Kalli laughed bitterly. "Of course he's guilty.

Anyone who's ever worked there knows he's guilty. The guy is a pig."

"No," I said, "the guy is a criminal."

Kalli shot me a look, then nodded.

"Sorry you've lost your job," I said.

Kalli shrugged. "Don't have to deal with his roaming hands now."

"Did you ever report him?" I asked.

"Never figured there was any point. It's just the way the world is." Kalli sighed. "For every Gill who goes to jail, there are two dozen more just like him."

As I drove home, I thought about what Kalli said. It didn't matter if she was right about the number of Gills in the world. I chose to believe that the world would become better than that. Many voices came out about Gill. Many voices would get him punished. Many voices could change things.

Chapter 20

We Too

It was another whole week before I felt the itch to work on some music. Without any plan for a song in mind, I used drum samples to lay out a beat on my computer. Then I searched my computer files for some old sounds I had never used. Sometimes a sound I'd forgotten could spark a new idea. I was free of dealing with Trey's lyrics. I could go back to creating the messages I wanted to share with people.

The music came easily. But I couldn't seem to think up any words for a verse or chorus. Usually I managed to scribble down something. Lyrics were like clay. You had to throw a big, ugly lump of it onto the page before you could shape it into something that sounded decent. But today my brain was blank. I had nothing more to say.

Or maybe I was too scared to put myself out there again.

It had never been easy to share my private thoughts with everyone in a song. After everything that had happened, I felt like I needed to protect my inner world. When I left the interview at the Java Shack, Ramead warned me that it might take time before I could trust people again.

Several attacks had followed the newspaper article. There were local music forums on Reddit, plus the Showcase's Facebook page and Instagram account, which nobody had pulled down yet. All of them were filled with hateful comments about the women who had come forward against Gill. Ramead was attacked the worst. I was shocked by how many threats she'd received. A few men threatened to rape her themselves. Other people made racist comments because Ramead was black. They spoke about her as if she wasn't even human.

But she was a hero.

Suddenly I got a burst of inspiration. A song about Ramead. A song about all the women like Ramead. Women who had the courage to speak out. A song about the power of voices to change things. About the power of voices to bring justice to the world.

About the power of my own voice to carry on my music.

All afternoon I worked on the song. I brainstormed clusters of ideas and words. I read online documents about the *#MeToo* movement again. I pulled ideas and feelings from those who had spoken out. I tried to capture what the movement was about. The real heart of it.

Then I started to piece together the first verse. Somewhere I read that, if the writer cried when writing something, it would probably make others cry to read or hear it. If that was true, this song would touch many hearts. Because I couldn't stop crying as I scribbled down the lines of the chorus.

I recorded the vocals. It was all coming together.

Then I got a better idea. I did another recording of the vocals, except this time I shot a video of myself singing the song. The instruments from my computer played in the background. After editing the video, I posted the new song on my YouTube channel.

I called it, "We Too."

✳✳✳

A few days later, Harold showed up at my house.

I hadn't told anyone about the new song. I wasn't ready to put myself out there that much. I hardly ever used my YouTube channel, and I only had a few followers. So I figured no one would see it.

"I saw your new song," Harold said. "Amazing."

"Oh . . . uh . . . thanks," I smiled. "Didn't think anyone would find it."

"Pretty awesome comments, too."

"What are you talking about?" I asked. "I have hardly any followers."

Harold laughed. "Well, I don't know how people found your song. But there are more than eight hundred comments."

My jaw dropped. It was something I read in books a lot, about people's jaws dropping when they were shocked. I never thought it really happened. But my jaw actually dropped open. I could barely get the words out. "Eight hundred?"

Harold looked surprised. "You haven't seen?"

I had spent the last few days catching up on school work. My nose had been buried in books every minute of the day. There hadn't been time for much else.

"Have you seen how many followers you have now?" Harold asked.

I shook my head. Last I checked I had thirty-four followers on YouTube.

"Seriously? You haven't seen?"

"No," I said.

"Ana, you have more than ten thousand followers," Harold said. "In three days. That's why I came over. What the hell is going on?"

"What? I don't know what's going on. Ten thousand?" I couldn't make sense of it. "That's impossible. It's got to be a technical glitch."

I sprinted up the stairs. Harold followed. In my bedroom I woke up my computer and went to my YouTube video. Harold wasn't exaggerating. I had more than ten thousand followers. I could hardly believe my eyes.

"How did this happen?" I asked.

Harold sat on the edge of my bed. "You might want to search the web. Search *Ana Santos*. And search *#WeToo*."

I opened a new tab and searched. A bunch of results popped up.

Young Musician Captures the Spirit of the #MeToo Movement.

It was a tweet that had been retweeted more than twenty-one thousand times. The original was posted by Ramead Ngozi.

So that's how this happened.

I went back to the YouTube page and read the comments. I braced myself, expecting to find at least some mean comments. But there were none. There was no room for mean words. Not on a page with this much optimism.

All the comments supported my message of joining voices against sexual harassment and sexual assault. Many also talked about what an incredible talent I was. A number of musicians offered to join the Shadow Beat band. There were requests in the comments for interviews and musical appearances.

Sitting back in my chair, I stared at the ceiling and smiled.

"You have that look in your eyes," Harold said.

My smile got bigger. I knew what he meant. He always saw the faraway look I got.

I was smiling because I still had a dream to chase. I would work my ass off and keep making music every day. I would sometimes sacrifice time with friends and family to pursue my career. *If those friends support me*, I figured, *they'll understand*. But it didn't mean lying or sneaking around. And it didn't mean trying to do everything on my own. No one made it in life without the help of others.

All I wanted to do — as Shadow Santos or just plain Ana — was to lift people up.

With my music.

Acknowledgements

Thank you to every girl and woman who has used their voice to speak their truth. *#MeToo.*

Thank you to Kat Mototsune and Carrie Gleason for making this book what it is.